THE ADVENTURES OF MONA PINSKY

THE ADVENTURES OF MONA PINSKY

BY HARRIET ZISKIN

CALYX Books ☾ Corvallis, Oregon

The publication of this book was supported with grant support from the Lannan Foundation and the Oregon Arts Commission.

Cover art by Linda Fire
Cover and book design by Cheryl McLean
with Micki Reaman and Carolyn Sawtelle

CALYX Books are distributed to the trade through **Consortium Book Sales and Distribution, Inc., St. Paul, MN, 1-800-283-3572**.

CALYX Books are also available through major library distributors, jobbers, and most small press distributors including: Airlift, Banyan Tree, Bookpeople, Inland, Pacific Pipeline, and Small Press Distribution. For personal orders or other information contact: CALYX Books, PO Box B, Corvallis, OR 97339, (503) 753-9384, FAX (503) 753-0515.

∞

The paper in this book meets the guidelines for permanence and durability of the Committee on Production Guidelines for Book Longevity of the Council on Library Resources and the minimum requirements of the American National Standard for the Permanence of Paper for Printed Library Materials Z38.48-1984.

Library of Congress Cataloging-in-Publication Data

Ziskin, Harriet,
    The adventures of Mona Pinsky / Harriet Ziskin
        p. cm.
    ISBN 0-934971-44-7 (cl.):$ 24.95 —ISBN 0-934971-43-9 (pbk.): $12.95.
    I. Title
    PS3576.I5758A65   1995
    813'.54–dc20   95-5303
                                                           CIP

Printed in the U.S.A.
9 8 7 6 5 4 3 2 1

I am grateful to Judy Grahn for inspiration and nurturing, and also to the women in her workshop and my writing group.

PROLOGUE

FORTY-FIVE MINUTES from North City, California Bay leaves its wide bed to pass through a narrow channel. Here gloomy warehouses and oil refineries hover over the water as occasional barges pass silently by. There is a damp sea breeze, and the smell of salt and sulfur.

Valley Boulevard runs south off the freeway, away from the water, across a wide stretch of flatlands and through Lexington City, where thick clusters of tiny stucco houses radiate out from an industrial core. It disappears into the folds of the nearby hills where houses are spaced farther apart and are larger. The hills are mountains really, old and worn, purple at twilight. At the crest, looking back, you see asphalt rooftops and then North City across the bay. Orchard Valley lies to the south, completely encircled by hills, once farms and ranches and apricot orchards set among manzanita and chaparral.

Years ago someone planted the hillsides with vines to hide the brambles and thorns, and now the dry, still air is filled with the songs of birds and the smell of jasmine. At the valley's center are concrete buildings marking the small city of Orchard Hills. Closer to the edges are a series of towns, bedroom communities, wood-shingled roofs dispersed among groves of eucalyptus and pine, connected by narrow roads, which loop through the hills, ending where they begin. Valley Boulevard on the north and Harrison Boulevard on the east are the only ways in and out of this valley. They are patrolled by sheriff's cars, which cruise constantly back and forth, safeguarding the borders.

PART ONE

1

THE TALL MAN is talking. Mona noticed him the minute he entered the restaurant, a phantom, one part of his long body flowing into the next, moving through the dark entryway and into the foyer towards her station. He said his name was John Shoemaker when she took his reservation, and she wanted to ask if they had met before, but he turned away so quickly she barely saw his features. She noticed his fine gabardine suit, the suede attaché case at his side, and at that moment she had the feeling she knew him, had known him when she was a child, although it was impossible. He was far too young.

Now he is seated with three other men in booth number one, and she is on a bench in the entry, inches away, sitting in semi-darkness, taking her break. He is in the booth he insisted on having, hidden from view by a carved divider. The distance between them is so small that if it were not for the divider, she would be able to reach out and touch him, she would be able to stare into his cavernous eyes. As it is, the divider is not as solid as it seems, it is hollow inside, and even over the noise of the lunchtime crowd she can hear him and his friends talking. She can hear attaché cases snapping open and papers rustling. She can hear the sound of ice cubes clinking.

One of the men mentions Victor's Grove, an executive development in Jasmine. She has lived in Jasmine for forty years. Another mentions Jasmine street names, Bonanza Way and Mother Lode Lane, streets she passes on her way to work every day. She tells herself the men probably are real estate agents. Probably their office is in Orchard Hills and that is why Shoemaker seems so familiar.

She stares into the foyer where waiting customers stand on Persian rugs and sit in filigreed chairs, men dressed in light-weight suits and ties, women in soft skirts and blouses. Off to the side an olive tree grows up from a hole in the entryway floor, its gray branches clinging to the stucco walls like slender fingers, mirror tiles overhead reflecting the tree's upside-down image. Her eyes close against the heat and the noise of the crowd, her chin drops to her chest, and as she dozes off the image of the upside-down olive tree remains, its branches so thick with red fruit they bend upwards, towards the roots, away from the crown.

Now from behind the divider comes the word "crime." It is a surly word harshly spoken that jars her awake, a strange word to be hearing if the men are still on the subject of Jasmine, where people move to get away from crime. They must be talking about Lexington, she thinks, or some other city along the Bay, but if that is true then why is one of them saying, "We should kick off in Jasmine Village where we'll impact more people," and why is Shoemaker responding, "The best game plan would be to start in the Jasmine hills. We'll have more visibility"?

She shrugs and stretches and is about to stand, thinking she has heard more booth talk over the years than she cares to admit, far stranger things, but now comes a whispered word "robbery" that she cannot ignore because there has not been a robbery in Jasmine for years.

She slides closer to the divider, and she hears Shoemaker saying, "To success. To a promising new venture," and the sound again of ice cubes clinking, and she reassures herself that, after all, these are ordinary real estate agents getting together to toast a deal. At this moment probably half the real estate agents in the valley are having lunch and doing exactly the same thing, but why are these men whispering again, and why is one of them asking, "Should we do it before or after Christmas," and why is Shoemaker answering, "J.C. wants it done before Christmas when it will be most upsetting"?

The four men must be planning a robbery in Jasmine Village or in the Jasmine hills, or is she mistaken, did she misunderstand? She would like someone else to listen in on the conversation. Sam, her boss, is across the entryway, but he is busy at the cash register making change. Perhaps there is time to run into the kitchen to tell Dorothy, but no, there is Sam glancing at the clock, signaling to her that her break is over. The next break is not until three and by then Sam will be secluded in his office, Dorothy will be on her way home, and the men will be gone.

2

Mona's one-room cottage in Jasmine,
that evening

THE CRESCENT MOON is reflected in the softwood floor. Mona sets her parcels in a rim of light that disappears when she closes the door.

Invisible, she hurries through the darkness to the far wall to switch on the TV. The flickering light accentuates her high cheekbones and Semitic nose, and it blackens the mascara around her eyes. She turns the dial past the football game and the seven o'clock news to the mystery movie. Disappearing into the darkness again, she crosses the room to the closet, unbuttoning her coat as she goes.

Ever since lunchtime, Shoemaker has been on her mind. The face she sees is blurred, she realizes, and she is no longer so positive that she has met him before. Still, the image of his stretched body is vivid, and the sound of his words is clear. She tries vainly to erase these unpleasant memories from her mind by concentrating on the TV. She tries convincing herself that her imagination is running wild, that customers always say strange things, especially when they are sitting in booth number one behind the divider and think they cannot be heard. But Shoemaker's words, "Do it before Christmas when it will be most upsetting," will not go away.

She sighs, reaches into the bookcase behind her for the telephone directory, and by the TV's light she flips through the pages until she comes to the *S*'s where, like a Ouija planchet, her index finger slides over "Scranton, Lucy" and "Scudder, Amos," stopping on "Shoemaker, John," a real estate agent on Canyonview Boulevard in Orchard Hills with a residence on Three Miners Drive in Jasmine.

She touches the print, closes her eyes. Perhaps the feel of the ink will be revealing. She sees cold, gray eyes (did he have gray eyes?) surrounded by short blond lashes, the moon sliver reflected at the edge of the pupils, a cloud cutting across the moon. Her body twitches.

She copies the two telephone numbers and addresses on the back of last month's water bill, which she anchors under the candlestick on the dropleaf table, a reminder to herself to ask her daughter Adina about Shoemaker when Adina stops by later for tea. Adina works part-time as a receptionist at the Jasmine Chamber of Commerce and knows the name of every businessman in the valley.

Mona pulls off the green silky dress she wore to work, untangles the fringes at the bottom. She slips into the terry robe

Adina and Adina's husband Gideon gave her last Christmas, which she does not particularly like because it hangs awkwardly over her full bosom and is far too long for her short frame, but it pleases Adina when she wears it, and Mona can switch into the lavender chiffon after Adina leaves. Lavender is good against her olive skin and steel-gray hair.

As she fumbles with the thick sash, she is startled by the sound of a man's voice crying "Go!" She glances at the TV where a lone detective is silently pursuing a criminal down an empty street. "Then who is talking?" she asks aloud. "Hello? Is someone outside?" she calls as she runs to the door. "Hello?"

Dark ruffles sail across the moon, the evening air smells of orange blossoms and pine, and all she can see are shadowy clumps of chaparral at her feet and an outline of the picket fence separating Adina and Gideon's house from her tiny cottage.

Back inside, she turns on the overhead light. Everything in the cottage is as she left it this morning: quilts and pillows neatly arranged on the daybed, cupboards closed. "You're hearing things, Mona," she tells herself. She hurries to the kitchenette to turn on the flame under the water. It is eight-fifteen by her Timex watch. Adina will be by any minute for tea.

"Go." The voice, thin, high-pitched, returns.

"Hello?" she whispers. No one answers. A window rattles. There is the troubling sense that she is not alone. "Izzy? Is that you?" Of course it's not. Izzy, her husband, has been dead for twenty-five years. It has to be the memory of Shoemaker's voice following her home.

If Gideon were here he would say she was imagining the whole thing. Adina has often said Gideon thinks Mona has an excessive imagination, and Mona has to admit there could be an innocent explanation for what sounded so suspicious. No one will ever let her forget the day the salami man came into Sam's, a little man who kept looking back over his shoulder as he walked in, even though the restaurant was deserted and there was nothing to look at. He walked in, his head turning back and forth, and all the while his right hand was pressed hard against his bulging hip pocket. Obviously he was carrying a gun. Mona casually stepped behind the bar to push the alarm and soon there were sirens and flashing red lights and when the police searched the man's back pocket they found a pound roll of Napoli hard salami. Sam said he thought the man had probably lifted it from Safeway across the street. It happened two years ago, but her family and friends have never forgotten. She would like to call Dorothy or Sam, tell them about what she heard Shoemaker say, but maybe she had better wait awhile, think it over.

She lies down on the daybed, breathing deeply, trying to make the voices and shadows disappear. On the wall ahead her Cousin Naomi's brass Star of David is surrounded by family pictures—Adina, Izzy, Mona's parents and grandparents looking so stiff and stern. These are things she barely notices anymore, yet tonight she finds that they hold a certain fascination, especially the Star of David, tarnished and dusty, and the photo of Uncle Gabe, her mother's uncle who visited the family often when Mona was small. Uncle Gabe sang songs, and he always seemed to have a joke to tell, although the photographer who took his picture apparently preferred him sober.

Again she hears the voice calling "Go!" and she has the distinct impression that Uncle Gabe's lips are moving. "This is ridiculous, Mona!" she says aloud. She hurries across the room to pick up her parcels, putting the eggs in the refrigerator and liver in Zebadiah's plastic bowl.

She realizes Zebadiah is not home. He should be, and she has been too preoccupied to notice his absence. She runs outside. "Zebadiah, you're supposed to be my protector," she cries. "Where are you?" but the only response is Elvis's barking next door.

"Kitty, kitty?" She looks for some sign, on Adina's freshly mowed lawn, on top of the fence, among the brambles and bushes behind her cottage, but nothing moves, not even the night bird perched on a branch of the lone eucalyptus, which is forever praying at the feet of the hills.

3

Mona's cottage,
a few minutes later

"'ZEBADOYAH, YOU'RE supposed to be my protector.' Mom, I could hear you talking to yourself all the way across the lawn!"

Adina stands in the doorway wearing Calvin Klein jeans, white running shoes, and a fisherman's knit sweater, carrying an enameled salad bowl. She tells herself she should be used to hearing her mother talk to herself by now, but the Torinos' house is not that far away, and what if they heard? Who could help but hear her mother's scratchy voice and the New York accent?

Mona goes to the stove to pour the tea. "I know I talk to myself, dear. People who live alone talk to themselves." She is suddenly aware of the arthritis in her hands and misses the cup. Water splashes onto the counter. "Damn!" Gideon is often critical of her and she does not like to think that sometimes Adina is too, so she tells herself that Shoemaker's long image, still in her mind, is making her arthritis act up. She tells Adina that she is worried because Zebadiah has not come home.

"He must have found a lady friend. He's very handsome, you know." Adina straddles one of the dining room chairs. When she was a girl her father carved an *A* on the back, so it is her chair and she is at home in this cottage. She grew up in the big house, where she and Gideon now live, and the cottage was the guest house then, a way station for relatives visiting from the East, cousins and aunts and uncles, all Pinskys who stopped coming after her father died.

"Maybe you're right," Mona replies. "Maybe he's horny," although Mona had him fixed last summer when he was still a kitten. She shrugs. "Stranger things have happened...he was restless this morning. Be careful of the chair, dear." She serves the tea. "How did your day go?"

"Oh, Andrew got an *A* in arithmetic and Ian got the lead in the school play, and Gideon's still at work—the usual." Gideon was not home until nine o'clock last night, ten the night before. He has just started his own architectural firm and is hoping to land the new county jail project, has been working steadily on designs. He says the job is important, not only because of the pay, but because the jail site is to be on top of Overlook Hill so that the jail will actually stand as a monument, a reminder to would-be criminals that the valley towns intend to remain peaceful and free of crime. He says the county can build a new hospital with the money it makes renting the empty cells to neighboring cities whose jails are filled, and Adina takes pride in his energy and his determination to make his place in the world. "The kids didn't touch the salad, so I brought it for you to nibble on before you go to bed," she tells Mona. "I'm having a horrible time getting them to eat vegetables. Gideon hates vegetables, and of course they copy him."

"How gorgeous your salad is, dear, so many different kinds of greens and such red tomatoes." Mona looks at Adina, at the shadows around her eyes. She always seems to be tired, and it is worrisome too, having Gideon working so hard, being so single-minded about getting ahead. Mona wonders if he ever has time for sex.

"They're quote, unquote 'vine-ripened' Mexican tomatoes."

"You could use the salad as the centerpiece for Thanksgiving dinner." Mona laughs.

"That would be a switch, wouldn't it? How do you like my new jeans, Mom?" Adina stands and poses. "Caroline and I went to Nordstrom's." Adina knows she looks beautiful. Everyone has been telling her how beautiful she is since she was small. She has Mona's olive skin, Izzy's straight black hair and turquoise eyes, and to everyone's relief she did not inherit either parent's Jewish nose.

"A curious thing happened at work today," Mona says eagerly, relieved to finally be telling her story. She pulls the water bill from under the candlestick and hands it to Adina, who glances down at the addresses and telephone numbers scrawled in pencil. "Tell me, dear, have you ever run across a real estate agent named John Shoemaker?"

"Karl Shoemaker is in Ian's class. I'm not sure, though, that his father is John. What's so curious about a real estate agent named John Shoemaker?"

Mona tells Adina what she overheard.

"Sounds weird. It sounds like they are planning something underhanded. Mom, are you sure you didn't misunderstand? You said yourself the restaurant was terribly noisy." Adina laughs nervously.

"I don't think I misheard, Adina. Does it sound ridiculous?"

"No. Just weird," although Adina knows Gideon would say it sounded ridiculous. Often he complains that Mona's imagination gets the better of her, that she watches too much TV, and once he told Adina he did not want his clients meeting Mona because they would find her strange. If he were at the table with them now, he would say Mona eavesdrops too much, she is always eavesdropping, on the bus, on the street, in the restaurant, Sam should soundproof the divider. Even with Gideon absent, Adina feels caught between him and Mona. "Sometimes your imagination does play tricks," she whispers. "Remember the salami man."

"Yes, well," Mona murmurs softly, trying to hide her disappointment. She is used to having her family not take her seriously, and usually she does not mind, but tonight is different. The image of John Shoemaker and the uneasiness it has caused are very real, and she finds herself asking Adina, "Isn't it strange that they were talking about crime in Jasmine, of all places?"

"Gideon worries that you watch too many mysteries on TV, Mom. He wishes you'd sign up for some senior enlightenment classes at Valley College." He wishes Mona would quit her job too, do something more respectable than working in a restaurant.

"I don't have time for classes," Mona replies. What is Adina thinking? She has her job, volunteers three afternoons a week at the convalescent home, helps Adina with the kids, "and besides, I'm not a senior, Adina. I'm a good two months short of sixty-five."

"I know. I'm sorry, Mom. Gideon's been working hard. You know how critical he can be." She squeezes her mother's hand, thinking how cute and round she looks wrapped up in the terry robe and how silly it is to worry that Mona might somehow stand in the way of Gideon's progress. Adina glances out the window, at the kitchen entrance to her and Gideon's house. Her eyes shift back to her mother. "They're planning an advertising campaign," she says. "It's so obvious. Like, they're businessmen. Criminals don't sit around in restaurants using the word 'crime.' These are real estate agents, like you said. They mentioned crime because their sales pitch is 'Come to Jasmine where there is no crime.' I mean, if they were criminals, why would they want to impact a lot of people? Why would they want visibility if they were planning a robbery?"

"You have a point, dear." Mona glances at the TV screen where the mystery movie is still in progress. Adina does have a point. Usually gangsters wear masks because they are eager to be invisible. Mona is relieved. She begins humming and soon she is singing "Remember the Salami" to the tune of "Remember Pearl Harbor," and Adina is singing along, and the two are laughing together, throaty, contagious laughter.

After Adina leaves, Mona scolds herself, "Maybe Gideon's right. Maybe you do watch too much TV. Maybe you should take a class," although as she changes into her lavender robe, as she unpins her hair and shakes it loose, lets it fall below her shoulders, she realizes that Adina did not explain why Shoemaker was so insistent about conducting his advertising campaign before Christmas, or why he would want an advertising campaign to be upsetting.

IT IS AN ECHOEY room full of cast iron and stainless steel, with an arched transom peering out over the entryway like a half-opened eye. A yellow light shines on Dorothy Michael who is wearing a chef's hat and a white coat. She stands at a chopping block dicing shallots with two large cleavers, humming parts of "The Anvil Chorus." Her skin is very dark and she is big—heavy and tall.

Mona bursts into the kitchen. "They're here again."

"Who's here again?"

"The men in the booth."

"Which booth?"

"Booth number one."

"Booth talk. You're taking up my time with booth talk, Mona?" In one of Dorothy's lives she is a mystery writer. She has three books published and ordinarily she enjoys Mona's eavesdropping because it gives her ideas for her stories, but today she is aware of the clock. "My sister Sally is driving up from Houston for Thanksgiving with six kids. I've got to get home to stuff the turkey and make cranberry mold and sweet potato pie, and dinner for Leon and Junior, and then this evening Alberta and I have a mailing to do for Black Women United—and somewhere in between I have to find time to go over my manuscript, which I have to get to my editor next week." Her cleavers click on the wood with silver speed.

"It can wait," Mona says. "They're probably drunk—I mean, talking about crime in Jasmine."

"Crime in Jasmine? Girl, they're drunk. You know nothing ever happens in Jasmine. Even shoplifters avoid the town, it's so dull. Maybe they're planning to hire criminals to come to Jasmine to liven it up." She looks up and grins.

"They're suspicious, whisper a lot." She tells Dorothy what she heard yesterday. "They're sitting whispering, now, this very minute, when the sound level is Pennsylvania Station. I heard Shoemaker say he's having Thanksgiving dinner at his hotel. Tell me please, why would Shoemaker have Thanksgiving dinner at a hotel when he has a gorgeous home in Jasmine?"

Dorothy smiles. She loves the way Mona says Shoemaker's name. "Maybe your Mr. Shoemakah had a fight with his wife." She winks at Mona. "Maybe it's a different Shoemaker. Maybe your John Shoemaker's not a local real estate agent. Maybe he's a developer from out of town, from Ohio. Girl, that would be something if he turned out to be from Ohio because the Lexington City Council is about to pay a Cincinnati firm three million dollars to develop the land around the Adobe reservoir." This is why Alberta and Dorothy are doing the mailing, warning the community.

Mona draws close, puts her hand on Dorothy's arm. "One of the men said he had spent the morning going through county records looking for the most promising areas—areas where no one is home during the day. He named Victor's Grove, Howard Estates, Shetland Farms...."

"Whoo—" Dorothy raises her eyebrows. "Where the fat cats live." Half the population of Jasmine is rich by now, Dorothy tells herself. Old-timers dying off, the young and rich moving in. Everyone knows the rich steal far more than the poor. That's how they got to be rich and, border patrols or not, someday the people are going to wake up and realize that their pristine valley is infested with crime.

"I have a special feeling about this one. I feel something deep inside, you know. And someone is talking to me. I mean I hear a voice, Dorothy." Mona is deadly serious.

"A voice?"

"Yes. That's never happened to me before."

"Oh, I hear voices all the time."

"You do?" Mona is relieved. "I was afraid maybe I was experiencing the first stages of senility, you know." She leans against the chopping block. "Last night I couldn't sleep. The windows rattled all night. The beams creaked. I imagined soldiers were outside trying to bang down my door—why would I imagine that? I never think about soldiers."

"Beats me."

"Then I dreamed that Adina and I were flying side by side through the sky. We stopped at a cloud to visit my Great Uncle Gabe who was playing a violin. He was standing upside down, you know, like he was a fly, or a spider on the ceiling—"

"Or a character in a Chagall painting."

"I don't believe I've ever seen a Chagall painting," Mona says timidly. She never went to college. Her mother did not think it was the feminine thing to do, so sometimes Mona feels self-conscious, although she has heard of Chagall, of course, has heard his name mentioned on the TV game show "Jeopardy." "Anyway, Adina left me and flew off towards the sun," she continues, "and soon she was a shadow I couldn't feel or see, a white shadow melting into the clouds, a white feathery figure wearing a white hat and white satin shoes—"

"That's Salome."

"Salome?"

"You're describing Salome. That's exactly how she dresses." Salome is a regular at Sam's, a street-wise woman who appears at the bar every afternoon at two-thirty sharp, for food, not for drinks. She knows Sam will feed her. Dorothy leaves work at three and always sees her.

"Of course it's Salome. Funny, I didn't recognize her."

"You often don't recognize people when you're dreaming. But it's important to keep track of your dreams."

"Important? Why?"

"Honey, you can never tell when the spirits are trying to get through." Dorothy wipes her hands on a dishrag and slips out of her chef's coat and hat. "I think I'll go out and listen to your suspicious men, just for a minute." She turns off the flame under the kettle. There is a loud pop.

"Did you hear that?" Mona asks.

"The stove acting foolish again."

"No, that's not what I meant—the voice."

"Just now?"

Mona nods.

"What did it say?"

"It said, 'Go!'"

"'Go'? That's all?"

"I think so. Maybe it said, 'You shall go.'"

"Honey, that's weird."

"I know it's weird."

"No, you're misunderstanding. I'm talking about Salome. When I saw her yesterday at the bar I could hear her muttering—you know how she does: her lips barely move and the words float out on little bubbles."

Mona nods.

"Mona, I could swear she was saying, 'You shall go.'"

GIDEON FAIRCHILD helps Mona into her chair, then stands at the head of the dining room table until his guests are seated. He is tall, has a freckled face, bluish eyes, and thinning red hair.

He smiles at Alex and Rosellen Lemay and Walt and Georgette Benston. Alex and Walt are his contacts in the county engineering department, the men in charge of the jail project, and Mona knows he is pleased that they accepted his invitation. Adina has arranged the seating with Gideon and the guests at one end, and herself and Ian and Andrew and Mona at the other, nine of them in all, an empty tenth space opposite Mona. Adina is the last to sit down.

The dinner party was Adina's idea. Mona offered to take the boys for the weekend so that Adina and Gideon could get away, but neither the Benstons nor the Lemays have family close by and Adina did not want to pass up an opportunity for Gideon to make an impression. Several other firms are bidding on the new jail, and small things sometimes make the difference. Eyes drop as Gideon leads the prayer. His basso voice rings out like an actor's. It is difficult to imagine that God does not hear.

Dinner is by candlelight, and overhead the spray of small white bulbs is dimmed, the chandelier Izzy gave to Mona years ago, a gift from Bronstein's where Izzy managed the men's wear department, one of the few physical remnants of their marriage. At Mona's invitation Adina and Gideon moved into the big house after they were married, Mona insisting she would be happier in the cottage where there would be less to look after, and over the years Adina has replaced her parents' mismatched Victorian with Helsinki Design and she has covered the hardwood floors with velvety carpets. Her Mikasa china looks almost liquid against ivory linen. A Gump's crystal bowl filled with late garden roses glows in the flickering light.

Gideon ends the prayer with "Thank you, Lord." He sits tall, smiles at his guests, announces that being here today, enjoying good food and good company, takes him back to the family gatherings of his childhood where his grandfather entertained everyone with stories about John Fairchild, an ancestor who lived five hundred years ago, a noble Scot, a man who rode on horseback searching for the highest hill in all of Scotland, on which he intended to build his castle. Gideon is an expert storyteller. He projects his voice effortlessly and dramatically and has the guests in stitches as he relates his ancestor's strange adventures.

Adina has served small plates of Chinese fishballs set on beds of cilantro. Seeing that Walt is having trouble spearing a fishball with a fork, Gideon interrupts his story to announce, "These are slippery little buggers. The Chinese eat them with their fingers." There have been drinks and pâté in the living room before dinner, so the atmosphere is warm and free, and after Gideon demonstrates the Chinese method, the guests follow suit.

Mona observes sadly as Adina blushes. The fishballs took hours to make. Adina learned the recipe just last week at a cooking class she and Caroline are taking at the Elegant Gourmet in Jasmine Village. Mona observes Gideon too, his eyes shifting quickly from guest to guest and the edge of the tablecloth trembling above his lap as his knee bobs up and down. He is a good provider for Adina and the boys, but she wishes he could relax.

Mona stands when Adina begins clearing the fish plates, then quickly sits down again when she sees the uneasy expression on Adina's face. Yesterday Adina told Mona that Gideon would like her in the background as much as possible, since this was more of a business meeting than Thanksgiving dinner. Mona does not mind. She is wearing an inconspicuous navy blue knit suit, her Sunday suit Dorothy calls it. She is used to Gideon wanting her in the background.

Everyone stops talking when Adina brings out the soup tureen filled with lobster bisque. Georgette comments that the scallion circles and bits of tomato floating on the top sparkle like emeralds and garnets. Adina's hair is freshly washed and it ripples, like the pale silk of her blouse and the black velvet of her skirt. Mona made the skirt, which hangs perfectly because it is cut on the true bias.

Alex smiles at Gideon in a way that says, "Congratulations on your choice of a wife." Gideon beams. Adina carries soup plates into the kitchen and returns with the turkey, which she sets on the sideboard for Gideon to carve. Gideon pushes up his shirt sleeves and hones the Braun carving knife on the sharpening steel with wide sweeps of his thick arms, as Adina carries out the remaining soup plates, returning with roasted onions, braised red cabbage, and brandied yams.

Throughout this procession Mona and the boys sit in silence.

"How well behaved your children are," Georgette says, smiling in Gideon's direction.

They *are* well behaved, Mona thinks. Even adults find it difficult sitting still for this long. God knows she does, especially when her arthritis acts up as it does now. She observes poor Ian grinding his teeth, a habit he inherited from his father. The muscles covering his jaws are throbbing like little hearts. It is hard being a child now. Parents expect so much, although it was not easy coming up fifty or sixty years ago either. Mona was also taught to make herself inconspicuous in the company of grownups. "If you call attention to yourself, society will frown," Ma would say. In restaurants she would tell Mona not to be noisy because "society doesn't like noisy people." At home, Mona was expected to keep her room spotless because "society doesn't like dirty people," and she was admonished to tie back her hair because "society doesn't like kinky hair." Society was an old sexless person who had big eyes and pointed ears and accompanied God on his daily rounds through the sky.

Alex comments on the lemon chiffon pie and Mona is pleased, since she stayed up late preparing it last night because it is Andrew's favorite.

"Gideon told me you worked in a restaurant. You must be the chef," Georgette says.

"Oh, how kind you are, dear," Mona replies. "No, I'm a lowly hostess—"

"Would you help bring in the coffee, Mom?" Adina interrupts, annoyed at her mother for describing her position in such disparaging terms, annoyed because Georgette is a real estate agent and Adina is afraid Mona will ask her about John Shoemaker, and how mortifying that would be. Gideon would have preferred not inviting Mona to Thanksgiving dinner at all, encouraging her to have dinner at Dorothy's instead, but Adina insisted. Her own friends enjoy Mona's company, she told him. They enjoy Mona's good spirit and sense of humor, although Caroline sometimes makes fun of the way she talks, and now Adina finds herself wishing the New York accent away, the way she says "deah" for "dear." Coming out of Mona's mouth, "lowly hostess" sounds so...lowly.

The boys race downstairs to the playroom, and Adina and Rosellen and Georgette take their coffee cups into the living room. Mona remains in the dining room, unaware of the tension she has caused Adina. Some things she does not allow herself to see.

As Gideon pours brandy for the men, Mona clears the last of the dishes away, and through the closed kitchen door she hears Alex tell Gideon that he thinks the state legislature has no choice but to pass the governor's budget, which means the county's building program will be slashed in the fall.

"My poor kids," she mutters. "What will happen to them if the supervisors don't approve money for a new jail?"

"I was expecting that," Gideon says. "I'm not worried, and I hope you aren't either. After all, if this job doesn't work out, I've got other irons in the fire." He sounds calm and cheerful, and she wonders how he manages the facade. Working alone as he does, he cannot possibly handle more than one job at a time. Just last night Adina was saying that he has been spending all his time on the bid for the new jail. How does he manage the facade when he knows there are no other irons and there is no fire?

"At any rate, I'm almost through with the sketches," Gideon is saying, "so I'll be ready when and if the money comes through. I've designed a spectacular tower. It will be fabulous on top of Overlook Hill. You'll be able to see it from anywhere in the valley."

"Sounds great," Alex tells him. "Stop by next week, will you? I'd love to see what you have, and you know even if this doesn't pan out, sooner or later we'll find something that will. You're young and smart, Fairchild. I like you."

"Let me tell you, I'm too good to pass up," Gideon replies. He laughs, then says, "Here's to success."

"Here's to success," Alex repeats, and there is the sound of the brandy snifters clinking as Mona starts the dishwasher.

MONA, WEARING ORANGE tights and a lavender top, bursts in through the double doors. "Three of the men are back. I've been listening in!" she calls out to Dorothy.

"What happened to the fourth one?"

"He must be hung over from Thanksgiving."

"Makes sense. Lord knows I am. I cooked up a feast for ten adults and sixteen children, and between the making and eating, Alberta and I stuffed a thousand envelopes. Stuffing turkey, stuffing children, stuffing envelopes. Lord save me."

"Dorothy, would you listen in for a few minutes? My break's almost over."

"I can't this instant, girl. I've got to get this chicken Cordon Bleu into the oven." She pinches her nose to affect the French accent.

"Booth talk again?" Sam calls out, but the women do not seem to hear, perhaps because of the commotion—waitresses and busboys streaming back and forth, the clatter of dishes. He does not care. He is used to being in the background. He is taking a break too, barely visible under a blue light, leaning up against one of the refrigerators at the back of the room, biting into a carrot.

"I'd love to know what they're up to. They mentioned Victor's Grove again, Mayor Hambly, said something that sounded like 'high turnout,' although that doesn't make sense when they're talking about real estate—"

"Turnout has a political connotation, and so does Mayor Hambly," Dorothy answers. She is too involved in her political struggle in Lexington not to make the connection. "If my memory serves me, Hambly fought off a developer's scheme a few years ago to merge Jasmine and Rancho and form a small city, so Hambly has a real estate connection too."

Sam takes another bite of carrot. Sometimes he finds Dorothy's logic far-fetched, although he has to admit to himself that strange things do happen. He listens with interest.

"That's something to think about, you know, the real estate connection," Dorothy says, laying down the cleavers. "Guess I have a minute to take a peek." Fondly, she pats a chicken leg, wipes her hands on her apron, moves a chair into position so she can climb onto a counter at the front of the kitchen and spy through the transom.

"What do you think?" Mona asks. "Are they too respectable for criminals?"

"Who says criminals aren't respectable?" Sam says loudly.

"Hi, Sam. I didn't know you were here," Mona says. "What are you doing hiding in the dark, acting like an outsider in your own kitchen?"

"I am an outsider in my own kitchen. Outsider is my middle name."

"Sam's right. Lots of criminals are respectable," Dorothy calls down from on high. "Most of them are, only often the respectable ones aren't called criminals." She waves Sam still. "One of them's saying something to Cherie."

"Is it Shoemaker, tall and swarthy? Does he have a long nose?" Mona asks.

"Isn't he fair?" Sam asks. "I could have sworn they all had short noses and were fair. I know just who you're talking about. They came in on Tuesday and cased my restaurant like they were looking for a hideout."

Mona blushes. She does not like to be caught making a mistake. "You're right, Sam. Of course Shoemaker is blond. I wonder why I remember him as being dark."

"It doesn't matter anyway. There are so many shadows I can't tell what color he is. He's bald. I can see the bald spot on top." Dorothy frowns, wishing she had better eyesight. "He's looking up at the ceiling now, lah dee dah, hasn't a care in the world—oops. I hope he didn't see me." She ducks.

"I hope so too," Sam mutters. "All I need is for the customers to find out what really goes on in this kitchen."

"Here's Cherie again, serving them up with four Bloody Marys."

"Four?"

"The missing man," Sam says, walking to the front of the room.

"They're waiting for the missing man," Dorothy says. "That must be why they look sort of grouchy, don't seem to have much to say to each other."

There is a long silence.

"My Thanksgiving wasn't too good," Sam says softly. His thoughts have drifted home as they often do during the day. "Dolores was pretty sick, so the girls and I bought a turkey platter at Safeway and took it to my Uncle Ibrahim's. His apartment is dark and musty, pretty depressing. I think a million spiders must live in those cracks in the ceiling. The girls watched TV in the bedroom while I listened to Uncle Ibrahim tell stories I've heard a thousand times before about the family home in Ramallah. He complained a lot too about Lorna wearing makeup at thirteen, and Patti wanting to be a singer. He said the girls were trying to lead me astray."

"That's what girls are for," Dorothy tells him. She likes Sam. He has been good to her over the years. Few Blacks live or work in the Valley and Sam stood by her when things were said after she was hired. He grew up in New York, has an accent something like Mona's.

"Tell Dolores I hope she's better soon," Mona says. "Adina had a wonderful party, but Zebadiah's been gone for three days now."

"That's the trouble with cats. They prowl," Sam replies.

"Cats and humans," Dorothy mutters. "Stop the chattering, you two. Here comes a man who looks just like Mr. Abernathy, the undertaker in North Lexington, only he's white." The transom is steamy from her breath and she wipes it clean. "He's handing a manila envelope to Shoemaker. Shoemaker's pulling something out of the envelope."

"Dorothy, maybe we should forget about this."

"Mona, what are you talking about? After all of this you want to forget about it? Come on, child. Get me my glasses out of the drawer next to the flour bin, will you?"

"Maybe you *should* forget about them and get back to work," Sam says.

Mona brings the glasses to Dorothy.

"Now hush, you two. I need to concentrate."

"I'm afraid to ask what you see," Mona says.

"It's a map, a huge one, looks like a planning department map, although I can't make out the details." Looking down at Mona, she says, "Remember when I used Junior's spyglass to spy on the phony ballerina? Look in there with the onions. See if it's still there."

Mona finds the spyglass and Dorothy pushes it up against her best eye. "I was right. It says 'Jasmine,' big as life. One of the men is circling areas in red."

"If they're real estate agents—"

"I thought you said they were gangsters." Sam finishes off the carrot.

"Looks like he's circled Bandanna something."

"Bonanza? Bonanza Way?" Mona offers.

"There's a lot of expensive ranch houses on Bonanza Way," Sam says.

"You know, I'm going to get a picture of this Shoemaker bird. I don't like his looks." Dorothy climbs down from the cupboard and starts for the towel drawer where she keeps her camera. "Mona, how about you going out and listening some more."

"How about going out and getting back to work," Sam says.

7

IT IS A SPANISH-STYLE building on a shaded street. From the parking lot the quickest way in is through the basement, down a dark corridor, then up the stairway where the rumble of the furnace gradually subsides, until there is a fluorescent hallway with small rooms on either side and the smell of urine. The hallway runs into a central lobby where patients slump in wheelchairs, heads quivering on long necks as they watch TV. Three other hallways radiate off from the lobby, forming a cross.

Mona hurries to the employees' restroom. She is wearing the African cotton she wore to work and carrying an overnight bag in which she has packed her costume for the Thanksgiving party—a turquoise skirt, orange jersey, and floppy green hat.

The all-purpose room is decorated with pastel crepe-paper streamers, and someone has set a cut-glass punch bowl on a long table. Mona makes balloon bouquets, which she hangs from the light fixtures.

David, an orderly, wheels in Lil Sternberg. Mona runs to greet her. "How are you feeling today, Lil?"

Mona knows Lil does not like being questioned about her health, so she is not surprised when Lil does not respond. Lil's parchment skin is almost the same color as her hair. A faded print hangs loose over her fishbone body. Mona wheels her across the room where other patients wait in a circle.

She tells Lil how beautiful Adina looked on Thanksgiving. "Someday I'm going to bring her here to meet you. She's never had a grandmother, you know. They lived so far away, and then they both died young. You two will get along.... It's just that she's so busy right now, and she's worried about Gideon."

"I was born in Cordoba, Spain," Lil replies. Mona has to bend down to hear.

"You were born in Cordoba, Spain? I didn't know that, Lil."

"I was born in fourteen hundred and ninety two." With her index finger, she wipes saliva from the corner of her mouth.

"Fourteen hundred and ninety two? That was a long time ago." Mona pulls up a chair and sits down. It is not always easy to tell how aware Lil is of what is happening around her. Maryalice Carson, the assistant director, thinks Lil is demented, but Mona sees Lil's detachment as a defense against being incarcerated.

"Baruch brought a priest to the house where my family lived for six hundred years." Lil looks down at her thick nails.

"Why would he bring a priest to your house?"

"My beautiful Baruch. My firstborn boy wore a golden cross around his neck, and his beard sparkled with baptismal water."

"He converted?" Mona asks.

Lil does not seem to hear. "The priest told my Reuben and me to go. This is no longer your home, he said, and when

Reuben refused he pierced his forehead with a silver sword. 'May God forsake you,' Reuben cried, and we fled to Germany where we built a stone house. We made sausages that we sold, but the priest followed. He told us to go. We fled to Poland, but there was the priest still, telling us to go. We fled to Russia where we lived under a thatched roof and bought flour and cabbage with the money we earned making shoes, but now Cossacks came and took our beautiful black-eyed Chaim. We prayed to God. My Reuben wound the phylacteries so tight around his arm, his skin turned white as the snow in Moscow." Lil holds out a trembling arm.

"What a sad story, Lil."

"I prayed to God for salvation, but what does God care? The Cossacks came for our last son, for our angel, Yankel. My Reuben and I flew away."

"Where did you fly to?"

For the first time Lil looks at Mona. "Cincinnati."

"Cincinnati? Aw, come on, Lil, you're pulling my leg. You really went to some romantic spot—Maui or Lake Louise."

Lil grins. She laughs. Coughs rattle her chest.

Maryalice enters carrying a brown bag filled with party hats and noisemakers, which she hands to Colleen, one of the nurses, to distribute among the patients. All eyes are on Helen Riley as she blows into her noisemaker, and there is a lot of nervous laughter as Stephen Lamott tries vainly to get the elastic string on his hat to stay under his chin.

Maryalice is blond and graceful. The flowing pink dress she wears makes her look like a fairy godmother. Standing outside the circle of patients, she waves at Stephen, blows a kiss to Helen, and before Mona has time to react, she slips behind Lil, pulls the wheelchair out and away, and wheels it to an open spot across the room.

Mona is furious. Maryalice always seems to deliberately come between the volunteers and the patients. She does not want to let this pass, but the orderly has just wheeled in Shirley Hilliard, whose birthday was on Wednesday, and everyone is singing "Happy Birthday." Now is not the time to make a scene.

"Dance, Mona," Shirley calls out. Helen claps. Mona moves to the center of the circle to perform a dance she learned from a Spanish dancer, a Sephardic Jew who was a customer at her parents' bakery on the west side of New York not far from Times Square. The dancer came in every day for a sweet roll. Mona's mother never liked her because she was dark and always wore thick makeup, but Mona knew she was going to grow up to be just like her.

Gracefully, she sweeps her arms over her head and stomps her feet. Her skirt twirls away from her legs as the full sleeves of her orange top become luminous wings. She bows towards Moses Segal, the director, who has just entered through a side door. He is tall and slouched and has long feet. Absently, he puts on a party hat. He nods almost imperceptibly at Mona, then circulates among the patients.

Colleen brings in a rectangular cake with yellow frosting that has "Happy Birthday Shirley" written on it in blue sugary letters. Moses helps Shirley out of her wheelchair so she can stand up and blow out the single blue candle. Colleen cuts the cake into small squares. Patients stuff their mouths and smack their soft lips.

With a curtsey, Mona finishes the dance. She sits next to Lil. Maryalice stands nearby, her eyes darting quickly from Mona to Lil and then to Moses across the way. Maryalice's head barely moves as her eyes spin an invisible thread.

"Watch out for Maryalice," Lil whispers.

"I know you don't like her, dear. She's a difficult person," Mona whispers back.

"Watch out for Maryalice. She hates Jews."

Mona's cottage,
Sunday morning, November 30

MONA HAS BEEN highly nervous ever since Dorothy climbed onto the counter with a zoom-lens camera "to preserve Mr. Shoemaker's face for posterity." The thought of having his face on film makes her feel somehow committed to an unknown course, and last night she had bad dreams. She wishes now that she had never laid eyes on him. She is sitting cross-legged in the overstuffed chair, eating potato chips from the bag, watching an old Thin Man movie.

Dorothy enters, waving a manila envelope containing two photos. "Girl, have I got news!" She turns down the sound.

"Not today." Mona is more upset than she realized and abruptly she runs into the bathroom, shutting the door behind her.

"What happened, honey?" Dorothy asks. Something must have happened because Mona usually enjoys solving mysteries and it certainly isn't like her to hide. Of all the times for her to get moody, just when this mystery is about to split wide open like a spoiled can of stewed tomatoes. "Think of what I went through getting the film developed." Maybe she can shame Mona out of the bathroom. Actually, Alberta's son Jerome developed the film in the basement while Alberta and Dorothy worked in the kitchen, stuffing envelopes. They were sending out flyers urging people to attend the next Lexington City Council meeting, and Alberta said it would be sinful for the council to pay developers millions to build luxury housing when there were so many people out on the streets. "Alberta says the Adobe Reservoir developers are the same ones who tried to consolidate Jasmine and Rancho a few years ago. Rodden, Mank, and Bullis," Dorothy shouts. "I told her I thought there might be a connection between them and what you overheard in the restaurant." Dorothy waits for Mona to respond. "Mona, are you alive?" She opens the door a crack. "Is it Moses, honey? Have you and Moses had a fight?" She cannot remember Mona ever being so mopey.

"No, it's not Moses. It's Shoemaker. His face is etched inside my eyelids." Mona stares into the mirror where the image of Shoemaker, smiling a Halloween smile, floats like a cloud behind her own reflection. "Dorothy, I've decided I want to forget about it," she murmurs. "I'm sorry you've gone to the trouble of taking the pictures." She wishes Dorothy would go away.

"If it isn't Moses it has to be Maryalice. She's done something to undermine you again. Girl, she's never liked you. I've said it before, and I'll say it again. She's jealous of you and Moses. She's attracted to him and besides she hates you for having an affair with a younger man—"

"She doesn't know about Moses and me, Dorothy. We're very discreet."

"She knows, honey. Believe me she knows."

"I don't think she does, Dorothy," Mona says, stepping out of the bathroom. "But that's not the problem anyway. It's what's going on inside of me. Dorothy, have you ever heard of anyone dreaming they were being born?"

"My sister Luella used to dream about that all the time. Why do you ask?"

"That's what I dreamed last night. It was a vision really. My parents' bakery was suddenly on fire. Ma was lying on one of the baking tables, and Pa was in his favorite chair, floating beneath the ceiling, above the flames—"

"That sure is some dream."

Mona nods. "I asked myself, is that what I have to do? Do I have to crawl through fire to be born?"

"Tell me, how did it go last night with Moses?"

"We didn't get together last night because he went to visit his cousin Harold in the city. We're having dinner together tonight."

"Oh, well, then I was right in the first place. It's Moses. That explains it."

"Explains what?"

"The dream. I always have weird dreams when I'm horny."

"When you're horny? When are you ever horny? Leon's home every night."

"Oh, Leon's home, all right. Usually he's so tired though he can hardly get his finger up to turn to the sports page, much less—" Dorothy and Mona burst out laughing. "But, come on, girl, I've got too much to tell you to waste my time talking about sex. These photos are about to burn a hole in the envelope."

"You know, Dorothy, I think that if I look at those pictures I'll never be the same again. I'm whatsherface about to be gobbled up by Jaws."

"Well, that there's no shark, girl. It's a bird. A jailbird."

"A jailbird?"

"Right. Here, let me describe the pictures for you and then you won't have to look. Okay?" She does not wait for Mona to answer. "They came out pretty clear. You can see Shoemaker's face real good, and one of the other men's. Shoemaker's eyes are set so deep in his head he looks like a skeleton and he has a weird mark in the middle of his forehead, must be a birthmark. But that's only the beginning, girl. I showed these to Leon yesterday, told him what you had overheard, and he thought we should call Joe Bourne, a legal investigator we know who works for a big civil rights firm, has access to all sorts of computers, you know."

"Oh, my god, Dorothy."

"Well, Joe called back last night to say he'd found him. He's John Shoemaker, also known as John the Shoemaker, also known as John Christiansen."

"John Christiansen?"

"You got it. He's on the FBI's wanted list. He's been convicted of robbery and burglary and now at this very moment he's wanted for breaking out of prison. Girl, we've got our man!"

Mona leans against the wall. She does not want to hear any more. She steps towards the TV where Nick Charles is standing in an enormous doorway inviting someone to come in. She wants to say, Dorothy, let's forget it, we've bitten off more than we can chew, but she cannot talk because a voice is whispering into her ear "go" or "go ahead" and she realizes that she is turning away from the TV and her hand is lifting a corner of the photo.

"Leon thinks we should call the police," Dorothy whispers, afraid that at any minute she will scare Mona away again, will send her back to the bathroom to slam the door and lock it.

"The police?" Mona asks.

Dorothy nods. "I didn't like the idea either, honey, but Leon is usually right about such things. He thought we should report that a dangerous man might be loose in the area."

"We don't know that he's dangerous."

"We don't have to *know*." Dorothy is feeling impatient. "We certainly have reason to be suspicious. If Shoemaker returns to the restaurant tomorrow, we can set up a tape recorder—"

"Dorothy, did you hear that?"

"What?"

"Fire sizzling," or was it Zebadiah scratching at the door?

Dorothy follows as Mona hurries outside. "Zebadiah?" she calls out, but the name dissolves into the fog.

"How long's he been gone, honey?"

"Four days."

"You might give them a ring at the pound, just to make sure."

Mona's eyes fill with tears. Zebadiah, Shoemaker, jailbreaks, the police—"I've called the pound every day."

Dorothy sighs. She is certain she has this man dead to rights, but clearly Mona is not up to dealing with him now.

"I thought we were just gathering material for one of your stories."

"We were. We are. Don't worry, honey. All of this probably doesn't amount to a hill of beans. We can talk about it again tomorrow, decide what to do then."

9

*Moses Segal's apartment,
late that afternoon*

"Hi, dear. Where are you?"

"In the john."

Mona has a bag of groceries on either arm. She uses her foot to slam the door shut, then hurries down a short hallway and into the kitchen. Over the radio an Italian tenor sings "*O Sole Mio.*"

Moses comes up behind her, folds his arms over her breasts. His hair, still damp, is matted against his scalp like dark oily feathers, and drops of water cling to his beard.

"Mmm, you smell good," he says, bending down to kiss her neck. She ducks and hurries to the living room window. Meeting just once a week as they do usually leaves her eager for love, and he is puzzled when today she dodges.

"What's up?"

"I don't quite know. I have to make a decision. I'm sitting on the horns of a dilemma."

"Sounds uncomfortable."

Ordinarily she would laugh, return the jibe. Today she is not sure in her own mind what she wants to say to him. There have always been things she tells Moses and things she doesn't. He likes silver linings, and their relationship is best when they are making love, or talking about making love, or talking, not too deeply, about the convalescent home. She is reluctant to mention the excitement and fear she has felt ever since seeing Dorothy's photos.

He knows something is wrong but will not press her. She will say what she wants to say in her own time. He insists that she respect his boundaries, and he does the same.

They gaze out the picture window at the Adobe reservoir, gray in the afternoon light, and at the barren hills behind it.

"Zebadiah's gone." She breaks the silence.

"Since when?"

"Since Tuesday. He must have a new love."

"Cats tend to be that way."

"I know. I'm not worried."

She must be worried. Why else would she raise the subject? He would never let her know it, but he is worried too.

After all, he is the one who found the kitten, a scrawny black thing, named it after Zebadiah in the Bible, King David's gatekeeper, although he is relieved to know that her moodiness is connected to something relatively small. "Why don't you have the boys ask around the neighborhood, put up signs?"

"I already have. I'm sure he's okay."

The cat probably *is* okay, Moses tells himself. Just wanderlust. "Have you heard the latest gossip?" he asks, glad to be able to change to a less personal subject.

She hasn't, and she too welcomes the gossip, respite from her worries.

He tells her that Colleen found Stephen fast asleep in his bed with Shirley. "She was half naked," he raises his eyebrows, "and there was the telltale empty bottle of Thunderbird on the bedside table."

"A little birthday celebration?"

He laughs.

"How did they ever get Thunderbird past Maryalice?"

"How did they ever get it, period, is what I'd like to know." Mona laughs as Moses describes the scene: Stephen on his side snoring, Shirley on her back, blouse unbuttoned, pancake breasts exposed. "Passion in Orchard Valley. It was a wonderful sight. If the home were full of Stephens and Shirleys, my job would be easier."

"Does Maryalice know?"

He nods. "I told her."

"And?"

"I guess she's worried about what the board will think. She'll recover."

"Maryalice always worries about what the board will think." Sometimes Maryalice seems more concerned about pleasing the board than taking care of the patients. She used to be different, Mona realizes. Her personality changed when the board passed her over to hire Moses, although it isn't worth the effort saying this to Moses, since he always comes to Maryalice's defense, says she is not jealous of him, she simply works under too much pressure.

Again Mona changes the subject, asking Moses how his day went with Cousin Harold in North City. Moses has no family to speak of, a few cousins, aunts, and uncles back east. He was married briefly years ago, but he rarely talks about the past. Once he told her he was born fully grown, an angel descended from the sky.

They met at the Thanksgiving party three years ago, the day he was hired. He was forty-eight then, just a few years older than Izzy was when he died, and Mona wondered at the time if this was why she was so attracted to a younger man. As for Moses, he confided that he was drawn to a dreamy quality he saw in her, and when he invited her to his apartment, she called Adina to say she was staying overnight at Dorothy's. Later in bed she told him how happy his lovemaking made her, although she realized that she still worried about being unfaithful even though Moses was certainly not the first lover she had taken since Izzy died. Moses asked to see her again the following weekend and they fell into a pattern of meeting once a week. She would have preferred meeting more often, but he said he had to have his freedom, that was his way, he did not want a consuming affair, and at sixty-one a woman did not bother arguing.

"The hills look like they must have the day God created the world," he murmurs.

She smiles. He is the only person she knows who thinks a lot about God and the Bible. Sometimes he even goes to synagogue on Saturdays.

Moses says, "You have to understand Maryalice's position—they're discarded, like old clothes, and she's supposed to make them happy. You see, ways have changed. My mother used to tell a story about an old woman she knew as a child who everyone called the Rebbitsen. I don't know why they called her the Rebbitsen. She was never married to a rabbi. They called her the dancer too, but so far as I know she never danced. She was old and she had no home, so people took turns looking after her. Who had nursing homes then? This was what you did. You fed her. You gave her clothes, a roof over her head. You never let harm come to her. More than that, you respected her, you respected her wisdom, you respected her age. It wasn't like it is today. When the old lady stayed with my grandparents, my mother had to be on her best behavior. To have defiled this woman would have been to defile the past, and that's what was different. Today's young people move fast, and if you want their respect you've got to keep up with them. Otherwise it's off to the nursing home. The Rebbitsen probably wasn't happy in her old age. I doubt, though, that she ever wore diapers, and this is what Maryalice has to live with." Too many patients wear diapers simply because the aides don't have the time to take them to the bathroom. Patients are embarrassed and upset at first. They learn not to care. "It's an impossible job and it's why she's not always so nice."

Mona hugs him. "Maryalice doesn't deserve someone as nice as you."

"But you do." He kisses her gently on the lips.

"Yes, I do."

In the bedroom they undress and lie under the covers. She rests her head on top of his chest where she can hear his heart pounding against his ribs. She pulls him on top of her to bury the sound and when they are through making love she holds him close. He is soft now but inside of her still.

THE SKY IS CLEAR and the weather forecast is for another sunny day. Mona decides to ride her bicycle to work, thinking the exercise will do her good. A second dream of a fiery birth had her running outside in her nightgown in the middle of the night to stare for a long time at the half-moon. At the same time Shoemaker's image returned. When she woke up this morning, she realized that she had promised herself to have an answer for Dorothy today, but had no idea what it would be.

She stuffs a scarf into her purse, which she drops into a plastic drawstring bag she straps behind the bicycle seat. She starts out cautiously on foot, tiptoeing her bike across the Torinos' backyard, trying not to arouse Elvis—or more visions and voices.

At Sutter Road, she mounts the bike and pedals quickly downhill into Jasmine Village, then slowly up Stage Coach Hill where the way is shaded by groves of eucalyptus and redwoods, poised overhead like guardian angels. Soon she is out of breath and she walks, brushing past bushes heavy with pink early-blooming camellias, stepping over orange calendulas and white calla lilies growing like wildflowers along the roadside.

Victor's Grove is ahead, built on land that used to be Bradley Victor's apricot orchard. The Victor's Grove sign hangs between two stone pillars at the Bonanza Way entrance. Burnt into the wood is an image of a tree in leaf, which, as she comes closer, she can see has been painted yellow. "Kids," she mutters. The thought makes her mad—kids did not do this sort of thing when she was a child—and she is aware of feeling uneasy too because Bonanza Way is one of the streets Shoemaker mentioned.

At the entrance she can see people standing in front of a house down the way and she knows something is wrong because it is Monday, a work day, and the street should be deserted. But there is Ray Niegarth, one of Gideon's friends, at the side of the road, examining a row of recently planted red-flowering gums, and there are Adina's friends Caroline Algren and Portia Twohy. Portia owns the Elegant Gourmet in Jasmine Village. Mona waves at them. When they show no sign of seeing her, she walks her bike past the pillars and down the narrow road. A pale sun stares at her from the side of the sky.

"How could anyone be so destructive?" Ray asks when he sees Mona. "Look at what they did." He points to a wide pink band circling the trunk of one of the gum trees where someone has cut through the stringy red bark and the cambium layer beneath it, so that the tree is certain to die. Similar bands are slashed into other gum trees planted across the road.

"This is so awful," Caroline says softly. "I don't know what to think."

"Neither do I," says Portia.

"The police just left," Ray says. "I don't think they have a clue."

"I don't know what to think," Caroline repeats. "I mean you expect the kid stuff—shoplifting, drag racing through Town Hall Park—but this is so cruel."

"It is," Portia agrees. "It's terribly upsetting."

"I've got to get to work," Mona says abruptly. She hurries off. Upsetting was Shoemaker's word and this is obviously Shoemaker's work and she must get to the restaurant fast to let Dorothy know that she has made her decision. Maybe the recurring dream helped to clear her mind, certainly seeing these wounded trees has, and she knows that if the men return to Sam's she will record their conversation, and even if they don't she will take the photos to the police.

"Go!" the voice whispers.

"I am going," she says calmly as she slips onto her bike. She pedals slowly at first, then furiously. The wind dislodges the pins holding her hair, separating the long strands into silver rays.

DEPUTY ARLO MALMQUIST, bathed in greenish light, is on the phone when Mona enters his cubicle. She can hear a man's voice coming from the other end of the receiver, and the murmur of voices in the cubicle next door.

"How do you do. I'm Mona Pinsky," she says after he hangs up. She extends her hand. He stands to shake it, and as he waits for her to sit down he notes the pouches of skin hanging underneath her chin.

She called Debbie at the convalescent home to let her know she would not be coming in today and then biked home to change into her navy blue knit, to show respect for the sheriff. She touches the gold chain around her neck. At the end is the silver star Dorothy wore to work that morning. "I want you to wear it, to ward off any evil spirits that might present themselves on your journey today," Dorothy said.

Mona has never had to deal with public officials before. That used to be Izzy's job, and now she relies on Gideon. Dorothy coached her as best as she could: Be assertive, she said. Let the officers know that you are hale and hardy and in charge of your faculties. Don't say, "Oh I'm sorry to bother you," and for heaven's sake don't say, "I know I sound crazy," and so Mona finds her deepest voice to tell the deputy she is the hostess at Sam's Olive Tree.

He knows the restaurant, of course. It has been in Orchard Hills for fifteen years. He seems like a nice young man, she decides after studying his smooth, clean-shaven face, and she tells him a little about her job.

"Do you want to tell me why you're here?" he asks her, smiling. He bets himself ten dollars that she will either say that she hears strange noises at night or that she sees menacing figures hovering outside her bedroom window. He is confident of winning, since most of the complaints he hears come from older women who imagine things because they have nothing better to do with their time.

Mona hands him a set of photos, along with a copy of the tape she made of the men's conversation today at lunchtime, and warns him that the tape is difficult to follow because the restaurant was noisy. She finds the deputy's smile pleasant, especially the crinkles around the eyes, and she is happy to see him open a notebook and prepare to write down what she says. No one has ever written down her words before. She feels somewhat like a college professor.

"So you think he's an escaped convict?" Malmquist glances at the pictures and drops them into a manila clasp envelope, which he closes. "See, you can relax. I've just locked up your dangerous man."

Mona laughs nervously, wondering if this deputy has an odd sense of humor or if he is making fun of her.

"Usually people stop by to see us because they are worried about noises at home—squirrels in the attic, you know. It's not every day we get an escaped con."

"Our investigator said he was an escaped convict," she hears herself answer defensively. She does not like the deputy's tone.

"We'll look into this, ma'am. We've got one of the best investigative units in the state." Malmquist says, still smiling. He drops the tape into a second envelope which he closes and labels. "Tell me, where do you live?" She gives him her address, he writes it down. "Jasmine is a nice community," he tells her. "You must have a big house."

"Oh, no. My daughter and her family live in the big house. My husband passed on years ago and I live by myself in the back house which is just big enough for me and my cat and the TV."

"I'll bet you watch a lot of TV." He winks, tears his notes out of the notebook and clips them to the envelope, which he tosses into a wire basket. "Well, I guess that's it."

Mona knows he is thinking she watches mysteries and gets ideas. He is just like Gideon. She never should have mentioned TV. What a dumb thing to do. She certainly won't tell him she thinks Shoemaker was responsible for vandalizing the trees on Bonanza Way.

Malmquist looks at his watch. "I'll submit this report to my supervisor and if he has any questions he'll know where to call you. Anything else we should know?"

She shakes her head, in her embarrassment drops her purse to the floor, and as she bends over to pick it up she hears a now familiar voice whispering, "Ask him who is his supervisor."

"My supervisor?" Malmquist is as surprised by the question as she is.

"Who will read your report?" Her voice is unnaturally stern.

"I don't know, ma'am. I've got lots of supervisors."

She starts to leave, but the voice tells her to be more insistent, and she turns back to ask, "How do I know who to call?"

He writes a number down. "Call next week. It'll take that long for a supervisor to be assigned to the case."

12

"WAIT UNTIL NEXT week! What's his trouble, girl?" Dorothy is furious. She tosses a handful of artichoke hearts into an enormous stainless steel bowl.

"I was so embarrassed when he talked about squirrels in the attic. He meant bats in the belfry." Mona has come directly from the Sheriff's: twenty minutes through rush hour traffic, then twice around the block because it's happy hour and Sam's parking lot is full. Dorothy warned her, she realizes, she should not be surprised, but not being taken seriously about such an important matter is an unimaginable humiliation.

"It wasn't anything *you* did, honey."

Mona is not reassured.

"You did just fine. You have to understand that the police are bureaucrats too, like everyone else. They don't appreciate outside interference. Imagine laughing at you, treating you as if you're a dotty old lady!"

"She is a dotty old lady," Sam says coming in from the dining room. He peers into the salad bowl, pulls out an anchovy.

"Now's not the time for jokes," Dorothy scolds.

It does not matter because Mona has not heard. "He wasn't listening to me, not really. He was pretending, you know, nodding his head, smiling, but his eyes were vacant. I know because I do the very same thing. Someone will be talking and I'll pretend to be listening when my thoughts really are a thousand miles away." Her shadow follows her back and forth, between the chopping block and the sink, as she tries to shed these unpleasant feelings.

"He doesn't like older women telling him what to do," Sam says. "It's a simple fact of life."

"Sam's right, Mona. He probably doesn't like Blacks either."

"Doesn't like Blacks? Oh, I'm sure it's nothing like that," Mona replies.

Sam bites into the anchovy, thinking how strange it is that Mona can be so smart about some things and so naive about others. She can add up receipts almost as fast as an electronic calculator, but in the seven years she and Dorothy have been friends Sam doubts that it has ever occurred to Mona that it might be hard for Dorothy to work in the valley, knowing how people feel, that they prefer Blacks as maids or chauffeurs. Numbers, yes, but facts like those do not seem to register with Mona who assumes that everyone is as benevolent as she is. Sam sighs. Maybe it is easier not to see, especially when there is not much you can do about it. "What's in the pot?" he asks Dorothy.

"Beef Bourguignonne."

"Smells good," Mona says. "Too bad I'm not hungry. I need a long hot bath." She watches Sam lift the lid to sniff the stew.

"That's a good idea. Relax tonight and tomorrow we'll plan the next step," Dorothy says. She spoons rice from a large pot into a ceramic bowl.

"I had the strangest dream last night," Sam says. "I, Samir Rafael Assad, was riding on the back of a dromedary and everywhere was sand, except that in the distance silver hills shone under a half-moon—"

"The moon was half-full last night. Did you see it, Dorothy?" Mona asks. "It was a gorgeous moon, hidden behind the clouds like a flower behind a chicken-wire fence—"

"We were sleeping in a tent," Sam goes on. He and Mona are talking past one another, she too shaken to pay attention to his story, he too absorbed in his dream to hear what she is saying. "Each of us was curled up inside an elephant-paw design on the tent rug," he says, "when our sleep was disturbed by soldiers shouting at us to leave and suddenly everything was on fire. The soldier was on fire, the rug, our tent, and I could see my grandfather Ismail floating above the flames. I wanted to go to him, but I was afraid to fly through the fire."

"You know, that dream sounds familiar," Dorothy says, but she is too preoccupied with this mystery to try to remember where she heard the dream before. "Soup's on," she mumbles and she sets the rice and a small bowl of stew on the chopping block as Sam pulls up a stool. "Maybe it wasn't your age, Mona. He could have picked up on your nervousness," she says.

"They don't like you if you're too confident either, especially if you're a woman," Sam tells her.

"It seems either way you lose. If you come across as too strong or too weak, either way they're going to find some quarrel with you." Dorothy reaches into the dishwasher for a dinner plate, which she hands to Sam. "Maybe I should go with you, Mona—to see the supervisor—"

"I think I should go alone," Mona says nervously.

"It's up to you. I just want you to know I'm available."

"I know you are, and I appreciate it. But I think I should go alone. I mean, it's sort of an adventure, isn't it? I'm whatshisface confronting the dragon—"

"St. George," Sam mumbles through a mouthful of stew.

13

MONA HAS NOT yet told Adina about her meeting with Deputy Malmquist, since Adina would tell Gideon and he would be sure to disapprove, but now as they hurry across the parking lot and into the mall and through the covered courtyard, the story flows from her lips like wine from a chalice. She is still so shaken by Malmquist's rebuff it is a relief to tell the story again—each time some of the fear and humiliation seems to leave her body along with the words. As she talks on, tiny white lights strung through the trees wait patiently, like luminescent spiders, for some unsuspecting prey, while in the distance angels sing "Silent Night."

"Maybe you shouldn't get involved in this one, Mom."

"Not get involved? But this man is a criminal, and look what he did to the trees!"

"Gideon says you have no proof Shoemaker had anything to do with the trees," Adina shouts. "He says it's probably just kids and he wishes you'd cool it."

There it is, just as Mona feared, Gideon speaking through Adina's mouth. Although Adina's response is not surprising, Mona is surprised by the anger behind it. She asks, "Is Gideon all right, dear?" Adina must be angry because she is worried about Gideon, and if not Gideon then someone else. "Did something happen to one of the boys?"

"Gideon's fine, the boys are fine. Andrew ate his oatmeal, and Ian grew half an inch." Adina smiles. "I'm sorry I snapped at you." She does not know what came over her, since she did not feel angry, the anger flew out of her like a being with a life of its own.

They are inside now, three steps away from the revolving doors into Macy's. Across the way is a plastic bench. "Let's sit down for a minute," Mona says. She takes Adina's hand. Nothing has gone right all day—the restaurant was mobbed, Sam was grumpy, and she tried for an early appointment with Malmquist's supervisor but Friday was the best his secretary could offer. Damn, there is the arthritis in her knee. "Let's sit down for a minute, dear, catch our breath."

Adina does not want to sit. She wants to go shopping. She went into work today and is tired. Next to taking care of Gideon and the boys, she enjoys shopping the most, and the sight of the Gobi Stein collection on the other side of the plate-glass wall promises her the lift she needs. She pulls her hand away from Mona's, slips into the crowd.

In the confusion, in trying to decide whether to sit down or to trail after Adina, Mona loses her balance and stumbles into the glass and chrome revolving door, which at this hour is in perpetual motion. She notices the man in the compartment behind her, tall enough and slender enough to be Shoemaker. It couldn't be Shoemaker, she tells herself, although she cannot be certain because the man is suddenly dark and, like a photographic negative, he is outlined in white. Her eyes have stopped discerning color, and she knows she is about to faint because this is exactly the way the world looked when she fainted in Marmelstein's Meat Market the first day she got her period. The revolving door has gobbled her up. There is no way out. She is circling around and around, bracing her arms against the chrome bar and her face against the glass so that her trunk is stationary but her legs are running. "Oh, my god, I'm a decapitated chicken," she cries out, terrified by the loss of control that this implies. Just as she is about to ask, "Why have you forsaken me," a hand touches her arm and guides her gently to safety. "Adina?" she whispers.

"Are you all right, ma'am?" is the reply, the voice of a man who helps her to a bench where, still blinded, she sits down.

"Oh, thank you so much," she hears Adina say.

When Mona's head clears the man is gone.

"He was an Arab," Adina tells her. "He wore a regular business suit, but the white Arabic headdress, you know." It is not every day, Adina thinks, that one sees a man in Arab attire in the valley. She must be sure to tell Caroline. She is aware of Mona's soft body beside her. "Are you all right? I'm so sorry."

"It wasn't your fault, dear. I tripped."

"I don't know what got into me, especially after Gideon's good news."

"Good news? Oh, I'm so glad there's good news. You seem so tense, sweetheart—I was sure something was wrong."

"I guess the reason I seem tense is that he made me promise not to tell."

"Not to tell what? Of course I won't repeat it."

Adina is silent.

"Come on, you can tell me, Adina. Adina, I'm your mother."

The angels are singing "The First Noel."

"Well, of course you shouldn't tell me if it's a secret. Let's go shopping, dear." Mona stands.

"I know you won't repeat it. I'm not supposed to say anything though until it's official."

"Until what's official—did he get the contract?"

Adina smiles uneasily. "No, that's not it. He didn't get the contract, not yet, but Walt thinks the votes are there on the board of supervisors to fund the new jail."

"Even if the state cuts the county budget?"

Adina nods. "It's close, four to three, and the swing vote isn't all that reliable, but Walt asked Gideon to quote, unquote 'submit plans.' Bison Tech's the only other firm he's asked, so it's a chance for Gideon to show what he really can do. My poor husband was up all night working on his tower design."

"Sweetheart, how wonderful!"

"Yes, it is," although Adina does not sound excited, and she is as aware as Mona is of the flatness to her voice.

"Adina, you look so worried." Mona has never seen Adina this way—worried, yes, when she has cause to be, not when Gideon is on the brink of success.

Adina shakes her head. "I've felt so strange ever since he told me. I mean, I'm not worried, Mom, and this is what's so strange, because I believe he'll get the contract, I really do. Gideon always gets anything he wants badly enough. The trouble is I'm afraid too—I don't know, I guess I'm afraid that now everything will be different. He'll be different, I'll be different. When you were caught in the revolving door just now, I thought you were going to die."

"Die? Me? I've got awhile to go, dear." Nothing that Adina is saying makes sense. Of course her life will be different, but that is what she and Gideon want, and obviously Mona is alive. "You must be afraid that something will go wrong at the last minute, dear. The swing vote won't swing."

"Maybe you're right."

That has to be it, although Mona herself cannot believe that anything could go wrong, and she wonders why suddenly now she is worried too.

All Saints Convalescent Home,
Wednesday, December 3

ARLINE MITCHELL, Lil Sternberg's daughter, follows Mona into the sunroom where a patient sits in a wheelchair alone near the window, laughing and cackling.

Mona leads Arline across the room to the kitchenette and invites her to sit at a plastic rattan table while she stands at the stove waiting for the tea water to boil. "I'm glad we finally ran into each other, dear," she says cheerfully. "I've spent a lot of time with your mother and I thought we could help each other to help her better. Would it be okay with you if we talked some?"

"Of course. How nice of you, Mrs. Pinsky."

"Mona. Everyone calls me Mona."

"It's nice of you to take the time. I know my mother can be difficult...." Arline fingers the buttons on her tweed skirt, wishing she had not agreed to the interview. It is hard enough visiting her mother, let alone talking about her.

"Oh, no. That's not what I meant. I'm not complaining. I like your mother a lot. I sense that we really get along. She's always telling me stories."

"I'm glad to know she talks to someone. She rarely says a word to me. I think she's angry at me for putting her in here."

"She doesn't talk to very many people." The tea kettle whistles softly. Mona fills a small stainless steel teapot and then sits across the table from Arline, a pretty woman in her late fifties who has turquoise eyes, something like Adina's. "Tell me, do you and your family live in the valley?" Mona asks her.

"No, we live in Lyme. My husband's a professor at the university."

"And you have children?"

"Two grown sons."

Mona smiles. "Grandchildren?"

"Oh, no. Not yet. The boys are both still in school. Bart is about to get his PhD in philosophy, and Wes is in a surgical residency."

"How wonderful. My daughter is grown. She has two sons too: Andrew is eight and Ian is ten." Mona takes a long sip of tea. "You're originally from the East Coast, I can tell from the way you talk." Her accent is Ivy League with broad sounds thrown sharply against the roof of her mouth, a different East Coast accent from Mona's.

"Yes. We're from New Jersey. We moved out here ten years ago and after my father died three years ago we encouraged Mother to join us—well, not join us really. We offered to get her an apartment nearby. We felt it would be better that way, you know...." Arline sets her cup on the table and sits stiffly with her hands in her lap, wishing Mona were more distant and less cheerful. She does not like seeing Mona, an older woman, wearing flowered tights.

"Oh, yes, I understand," Mona is saying. "And I'm sure your mother was happy for her independence too. God knows, the last place I'd want to live is in my daughter's house." Mona laughs.

"Mother was always active in her temple in New Jersey. I'm not religious. My husband isn't Jewish, but it seems to mean a lot to her, at least it did then."

"I know how you feel. I'm not very Jewish either. I wonder, do you think it bothers your mother to be in a Gentile convalescent home?"

"Oh, no. I'm sure that doesn't bother her at all. After she moved out here she aged so. Most of the time I don't think she knows where she is." She laughs self-consciously, thinking that may have been the wrong thing to say.

"Oh, well, I just thought—"

"After she moved here things began happening and the doctor said it wasn't safe for her to live by herself."

"Things?"

"Yes. One day she was on her way to our house. Usually she took the bus. I guess it must have been a nice day because she walked. She tripped over a crack in the sidewalk and fell and broke her nose. It happened in front of the Kayeds' house—he's chairman of the English department."

"How frightening that must have been—for both of you."

"Yes, it was, and a little embarrassing too." Arline is talking fast, taking small sips of tea between sentences. "Once she left her apartment to go shopping two blocks away. She ended up in Lyme Square not knowing where she was. Elmer Churchill, my husband's colleague, saw her. He realized she was disoriented, brought her to our house, so sweet to have bothered. Then in the middle of a dinner party at our house she tried lighting our electric stove with a match, nearly set fire to the kitchen."

"You caught it in time?"

"Luckily none of the guests saw. I confided to a friend, and she suggested a nursing home. She had her mother in one, said it was the best in the area, it wasn't as awful as people say. We felt terrible, we really did, but we couldn't have these things happening."

"Old age is hard, for everyone involved. I've been volunteering here for ten years. I know. All the alternatives are bad, although maybe some are less bad. Breaking your nose may be easier to bear than wearing diapers, you know."

"What are you saying, Mrs. Pinsky?"

"What I'm saying is this...." What Mona wants to say is that patients often get worse once they are in the nursing home, lose their self-confidence, some even forget who they are. Of course she would not say this to Arline, and she searches her mind for a gentle way to let Arline know that living in a nursing home is not necessarily the best alternative for Lil. "Here, let me tell you a story," she finally says. "Once your mother and I were in the sunroom when Stephen Lamott came in with his great-granddaughter. Actually it was the child who was leading him by the hand. She was a gorgeous little girl, five or six, I guess, blond curls, and she was wearing a St. Joan's T-shirt, a bright yellow shirt, and your mother was in her wheelchair, over there by the door. I was putting on the water for tea, so I was close enough to hear the child asking, 'Would you give me a ride?' Well, Lil looked very glum, you know how she can be. She dug her chin into her chest and refused to answer. The child sat down on the floor and stared up into Lil's face until Stephen got all fidgety, said he wanted to go outside. Lil glared at him and said, 'Hold your horses,' and she suddenly looked up and whispered to the little girl, 'I'll give you a ride someday, but you have to wait until I learn to drive better.'"

"My mother's always had a sense of humor."

Mona realizes that Arline is looking past her. She turns to see Maryalice, wearing a white uniform, walking away from the doorway. "I wonder what she wanted," Mona says half aloud. Maryalice always seems to appear at inopportune times.

"You know," Mona goes on, "once I was reading to a patient and Lil was waiting to be fed and I told her I'd help her as soon as I finished the page. A second later I happened to look up and saw her feeding herself quite well, thank you. She let the spoon drop to the floor as soon as she realized that I was looking. I think she was afraid I might disapprove of her independence. Of course I told her I didn't—"

"Our doctor says she has Alzheimer's. She needs constant care. We can't afford a private nurse, and I don't feel it would work having her live with us—"

"No, I'm not suggesting that. I'm not suggesting anything, really," although she wants to say that Dr. Engleberger and Moses both disagree about the Alzheimer's. They think Lil's depressed, and Mona thinks Lil would be less depressed if she lived in her own apartment. She doesn't need a private nurse, just people to look in on her. She smiles at Arline whose black hair is turning silver, as Mona's was ten years ago, as Adina's will be someday.

Again Arline sees Maryalice in the doorway. "I think she wants to talk to you."

"Oh, I'm sure it can wait."

"That's okay, Mrs. Pinsky. I've got to get going anyway." Arline is grateful for the interruption. Mona follows her out of the sunroom, watches her walk down the hall, past Lil's room and out into the lobby.

Mona approaches the nurses' station where Maryalice is bent over the desk filling out forms. Without looking up, Maryalice says, "I think it's best to let the social workers meet with the patients' families."

"I'm not meeting with her," Mona replies. "Just talking to her as a friend. Moses said it was all right for me to talk to her."

"I'm sure he did, but of course that doesn't matter now."

"What doesn't matter now?"

Maryalice does not answer. She walks quickly down the hallway and out the double doors.

"Damn you, lady," Mona says under her breath. She enters Lil's room where the lights are out and the blinds are drawn and Lil is lying in bed, staring up at the ceiling.

"Hi, Lil."

Lil doesn't respond.

"I'm so mad at Maryalice I could spit." The air is hot and steamy. Mona opens the window and raises the blinds. "I'm mad at myself too. I sounded like a child. 'Moses said I could do it.' A stupid child." She looks down at Lil. Poor Lil. What is she feeling inside? "So what else is new, huh?" She pulls Lil up in the bed, plumps the pillow. "I got stuck in a revolving door last night. Couldn't find a way out. Thought I was trapped forever, like a dinosaur in a tar pit, but naturally a handsome man rescued me. I think he was a sheikh."

Lil is barely breathing.

Mona whispers in her ear. "Lil, I think a ghost has invaded my house. Someone keeps talking to me. Do you know what I mean? Someone's talking and no one's there? There's a spirit about, you know. I think it might be the ghost of my Great Uncle Gabe."

Lil shifts to her side and squints up at Mona. "Does he have a Yiddish accent?"

Mona can hardly hear her. "A Yiddish accent? Who ever heard of a ghost with a Yiddish accent. Come on Lil, you're pulling my leg."

Lil smiles. Her thick lips part as she coughs up a laugh. It is a diabolical laugh that rattles the sides of her bed and spins drops of drool onto her jowls.

Mona reaches for a Kleenex on the night table. Lil restrains her.

"I was only going to get a tissue, dear."

Lil tightens her grip on Mona's arm. "It's Christmastime. Evil spirits are about," she says. With her free hand she wipes her face.

 15

"I KNOW SOMETHING about this case," Deputy Malmquist's supervisor begins.

Mona waits as he lights his cigarette. Shoemaker has not been at the restaurant since Tuesday. Either he and his friends have completed their work or they have decided to conduct their business somewhere else. "Apparently Deputy Malmquist didn't take me seriously," she tells the supervisor, surprised by her boldness. "I want you to understand I am not a crackpot. On TV they tell you to report anyone you see behaving suspiciously, and that is what I have done." She leans forward.

"And you did the right thing, ma'am."

Mona studies his eyes. They are brown and warm. She is inclined to trust him, but she knows she can be too kind in her judgments of people, a little gullible. Izzy always told her that, and so have Dorothy and Sam. "What would you think if you heard four men talking about crime in Jasmine?" she continues. "My daughter thinks they're planning an advertising campaign, although you can see her theory simply doesn't hold water—I mean, why would they want to upset people they were trying to sell to?" She tells the supervisor she considered the possibility that she misheard the conversation, until Dorothy listened in for a while and heard the same sorts of things. "I didn't want to involve the police though until I was completely sure. And here," she rummages in her purse, "yes, here's a statement from Dorothy Michael, our master chef."

"Very good." Deputy Malmquist's supervisor glances at the paper before slipping it into a file folder on his desk. "You were right to report it, Mrs. Pinsky. You did absolutely the right thing, and I thank you. It sounded suspicious to us too, and I want you to know we checked it out."

"Well, I'm relieved to know that." She *is* relieved. The supervisor must have overruled Deputy Malmquist, or could it be that Deputy Malmquist was not making fun of her after all? Not likely, she tells herself. She asks the supervisor, "What did you find?"

"We found this." The supervisor opens the file folder. "First of all the John Shoemaker in the pictures you gave us isn't John Shoemaker the real estate agent in Orchard Hills."

"He isn't? Well, who is he?"

"I don't know. We know he isn't the real estate agent because one of our deputies bought a house from Shoemaker and knows his face. Now, Shoemaker's a common name. There are about five John Shoemakers in the area, and of course he could come from some other city or state."

Mona nods.

"We could check out the Shoemakers in the area, but, ma'am, we have another problem. We obtained information about your John Shoemaker from the FBI, along with a mug shot—"

"Mug shot?" This is no salami man.

"Yes. And our technicians blew up your snapshots and they compared the man you identified as Mr. Shoemaker to the man in the mug shot, and in their opinion they could be the same man. The shape of the head is the same, although the mouth and eyes seem different. Your photo is too vague to allow us to make a positive identification."

"Did you try to find him?"

"Yes, we did, and here's what I mean. John the Shoemaker was picked up by the Cincinnati police on Tuesday. Now, that doesn't mean you didn't see him in Orchard Valley last week, I realize. I wonder though, if he was involved with these men as you say, why would he leave this area?"

"Yes," she says, she understands, although now she is uneasy again because she had thought the supervisor was about to take the case, but now she hears him saying he isn't interested. "Isn't it possible that Shoemaker has a deal going in Cincinnati too? Maybe his family lives in Cincinnati, maybe his wife is sick."

"Anything's possible. Mrs. Pinsky, you and I can speculate until the cows come home and it won't do any good. We have to have something concrete connecting your Mr. Shoemaker to a crime. Right now all we have is a crime that hasn't been committed and the suspect in jail at this very moment for doing something else. Look at it from our side. We are a small department. We don't have the manpower to follow such a slim lead. And even if we did, if we went poking around with such skimpy evidence, we'd be sued for harassment."

16

MONA IS GLAD she took her car because the air is cool. Last night she oiled her bike, polished it until it shone like her mother's silver teapot. She set it in Adina's garage to hibernate for the winter.

She waits for the engine to warm before driving to the shopping mall down the street, to Pedrocelli's Delicatessen for bread. Afterwards she will stop by Dorothy's to report on her meeting with Malmquist's supervisor. The three-quarter moon projects swinging shadows of tree branches onto the pavement.

It is almost nine so most of the shops are closed, although the lights are on and Mona can see the merchants still inside, rearranging stock for the Christmas crowds. Pedrocelli's is across from Safeway, between Tina's Dresses and Bulldog Shoes, its window decorated with sausages hanging in chains from the ceiling and huge two-hundred-pound imported cheeses. She hums "Remember the Salami."

Oddly, her spirits are high. Malmquist's supervisor certainly did not tell her what she wanted to hear, but she realizes that deep down she is relieved that he does not think he has a case, since her life can now return to normal.

Even at this hour there is a crowd inside Pedrocelli's where it is bright and warm and all around are smells of pickled meats and cheeses and olives and marinated mushrooms and lasagna and pasta salad and fresh baked rolls. Mona picks out two sourdough rolls before taking a number from the red dispenser. The wall behind the counter is covered with mirrored tiles so that looking straight ahead she can see the restaurant section, which is outfitted with glass tables and wrought-iron chairs. Four men are at the very back of the room, clad in pale gabardine business suits, all huddled over a table so that she cannot see their faces.

"What'll it be, Mona?"

"Hi, Louie. I'll take everything."

He laughs.

"Well, on second thought, I'll just take a quarter of a pound of pastrami and these rolls. I'll be back on Monday for the rest. My boyfriend and I are going to North City for a picnic tomorrow."

"Now what's a nice lady like you doing with a boyfriend?"

"Oh, some of us never learn."

Mona continues staring into the mirror as she waits for Louie to wrap the rolls. One of the men seems to be handing something to the others. "Looks like envelopes," she murmurs.

"Envelopes?" Louie asks. He hands Mona her change.

"Oh, don't mind me." Mona flushes, a little embarrassed to be caught talking to herself.

She drops the coins into her purse, glances into the mirror again before turning to leave. She sees that the man who was handing out the envelopes is now standing. He is tall and thin and she actually shudders when he turns because there is no mistaking the wide mouth and shadowy eyes of John the Shoemaker from Cincinnati.

17

"So, TELL ME, how can he be in jail in Cincinnati and in Pedrocelli's Delicatessen at the same time?" Mona is breathless from the climb up the back steps to Dorothy's flat. Dorothy, in an African print, and Leon and Sam, in Levis and turtleneck T-shirts, are at the kitchen table drinking coffee by candlelight.

"That is the question, honey. Come on in, get a cup of coffee, and sit yourself down." Dorothy had a feeling Mona would be by. Sam blew in from out of nowhere just a few minutes ago, and there has been weirdness in the air all day. "You know, it doesn't surprise me that John the Shoemaker's reappeared, or that the sheriff didn't buy our story. I'll tell you, Salome came by today after you left. She came leaping across the dining room, swimming through the air like a Genie rising from a teapot. So anything bad or strange happening today doesn't surprise me a bit, because it always does when Salome makes an appearance—I put sugar in the vichyssoise, or the osso bucco burns, or the sheriff has reasonable-sounding excuses. I swear, sometimes I wonder if Salome's real, you know. She's always wearing the same fluffy white dress and it's always spotless. How does she keep herself so clean?"

"She isn't real. She's an illusion," Sam says. Everything in life is an illusion. Here he is at Dorothy's kitchen table, not at home as he should be. This is his family. At this moment Dolores and the girls are memories. He must bite his thumb to prove he exists. The shadows on the wall are trembling in the candlelight—his, Dorothy's, Mona's, Leon's—even though everyone at the table is perfectly still. Which is real? he wonders, the object or the shadow?

"You know, from a distance, when you can't see the brown spots or wrinkles, she looks dreamy, sort of ageless," Dorothy says. "Sometimes she actually looks young. I once asked her how she did it, and you know what she told me? She said, 'Every thirty years I die and then I'm reborn again.'"

"She's nuts," Leon says into his cup.

Dorothy takes a pad of paper from the top of the refrigerator. The dinner dishes are washed and put away. Her footsteps are heavy and the room sounds empty.

"Forget Salome, will you? I'm asking how can Shoemaker be in jail in Cincinnati and in Pedrocelli's at the same time?" Mona is desperate.

"He's not in jail, doll. The police are lying," Leon says quietly.

"Why would they lie?"

"Why wouldn't they?" Sam says.

Leon gathers up his tall body to walk gracefully across the room and stand in semi-darkness pouring himself another cup of coffee.

"They definitely could be lying," Dorothy says. "That's a definite possibility. A definite possibility. But, let's do this. Let's write down all the possibilities so we can rule them out one by one. That way we'll know just where we are."

"Ah, come on, girl. This isn't one of your novels." Leon sits down.

"I'm aware of that."

Mona jumps up and hurries to the stove for more coffee. Everyone is talking nonsense. She wishes Dorothy and Leon would save their bickering. A few hours ago everything seemed so simple. The police were going to take charge, or they weren't, but either way her life was going to return to normal. Now it is as if someone has set a map in front of her and is marking new roads with infinite forks and branches for her to follow.

"They could have the wrong man," Sam offers. They always capture the wrong man, the police do, soldiers do. It does not matter what he has or has not done, so long as they can put him behind barbed wire and call him the enemy.

Dorothy writes down: "They could have the wrong man."

"How could they have the wrong man when they've got mug shots and finger prints?" Mona asks.

"That's easy," Leon breaks in. "They don't bother to check. Man, they pick up some poor beggar, some poor sonofabitch who's sleeping on the street, you know, messing up their downtown, an incongruous creature."

Sam nods. He appreciates Leon's perceptiveness, the way he thinks.

"I guess you're right, Leon. I imagine that sort of thing happens all the time." Mona sighs. She has never thought about jails or the police in this way before.

"Okay. Now, here's another possibility. Mona could be wrong. It wasn't Shoemaker in Pedrocelli's—"

"But I'm not wrong, Dorothy! How can you say that?"

"No, no, that's not what I'm saying at all. I'm not saying you are wrong, honey, just that it's possible. We have to consider everything, you understand? Sometimes you can mistake people. It happens. Mistaken identity. You feel certain even though you're wrong."

Mona shakes her head. She was not mistaken.

"Mona's not wrong. It's far more likely that the supervisor is lying," Leon says. "I think he *knows* the Cincinnati police don't have anyone named Shoemaker."

"Why would he lie?" Mona would almost rather be mistaken about the man in Pedrocelli's than to find that, despite her caution, she had been taken in by Deputy Malmquist's supervisor.

"Police lie," Leon tells her. "They don't want you messing around in their business. They do things their way, and they don't want questions asked."

"You could call the Cincinnati police yourself and ask them if they've got Shoemaker in custody," Sam suggests.

"Or better yet, we could ask Joe Bourne to check it out," Dorothy says to Sam, and then to Mona, "If they tell him he's not there, then we can feel more certain that he's the man you saw tonight. If they say he is there, we're back where we are now, with the same possibilities."

"If they say he's there," Leon says, "they're lying. And if they're lying, they're cooperating with the sheriff's office."

"Leon's right," Dorothy says. "The sheriff probably wants you out of the picture. Possibly he's been bought off by Shoemaker, or by the Lexington City Council."

"The Lexington City Council? Why are you talking about the Lexington City Council at a time like this?" Mona hurries to the stove for a third cup of coffee. Her shadow bounces across the ceiling and then disappears as she moves from candlelight into darkness.

Later that night

SHE DREAMS SHE is at the edge of a dark forest, riding a silver wheelchair, whizzing towards the darkness of the trees, as wind swirls beneath her turquoise skirt and tugs at her purple hair.

The ground boils and reeks of frankincense and a cat screeches and she turns back in fear, but Lil Sternberg's hand reaches out from behind a rotten tree trunk to grab her by the collar.

High above, where treetops are clouds, Uncle Gabe sits on a milk stool playing his violin while Lil sings words to the minor tones: "Duma is at my right. Mefathiel is at my left. Aniel is at my feet. Lilith is at my head." The words cling to mossy bark.

Lil wraps her arms around the tree and shakes the trunk until a thousand apples burst into flame and light the forest.

"You must," Uncle Gabe whispers.

Mona grabs a burning branch and climbs up into the tree.

RIDING ALONG THE freeway she tells Moses about Shoemaker. All morning she has been wondering what will happen if Leon's friend discovers that Shoemaker is not in jail, that the police are lying. What will it mean, what will she be asked to do next? She had not planned on involving Moses, but she is upset.

She is not surprised when Moses's initial response is to shrug. She knows he is not saying he is bored or disinterested, rather that he is overwhelmed.

He stares at the road, thinking that either Mona's imagination has run wild or it hasn't, and he cannot decide which possibility is worse, or what to say, and so he says what first comes to mind: "You see, the police can't lock someone up simply because he's suspicious. They have to have solid evidence."

"But photographs and tapes are solid—"

"And if your Mr. Shoemaker's in jail, how can he be in the delicatessen? Do you want the Jasmine County Sheriff combing the entire state for a man they think's already in jail, randomly arresting tall blond men? Next thing you know it will be suspicious Blacks, or people with AIDS, or socialists, or Democrats, or Jews."

Mona sighs, sorry she raised the subject. She is relieved to see the Mint Street exit coming up, knowing that they will not be able to talk for a while, since finding a parking space will require all their attention.

The sun shines over their shoulders as they walk down the street, while overhead is a filmy full moon. She tells him about her dream last night and Lil's strange song. "I'm almost sure those odd-sounding names are the names of angels," he tells her. "If I remember correctly, Mefathiel is an angel who opens doors."

They fall into silence.

"I'm thinking," Moses finally says. "You mentioned this man John Shoemaker. Isn't Shoemaker one of your family names?" He sounds more like himself.

"Schumacher." She pronounces it the German way. "My mother was Lena Schumacher."

"Strange coincidence, isn't it? Then life is full of strange coincidences, although if I were a rabbi, I'd seek the mystical meaning in the convergence of the two names at this point in time. The shoemaker has meaning for us Jews, you see. There is the myth of the Wandering Jew, where Jesus, carrying the cross, stops to rest at a shoemaker's house. The shoemaker sends Jesus away and Jesus retaliates with a curse, saying the shoemaker shall go, and ever since the shoemaker has had to roam the earth. He cannot die. He cannot find peace. This legend has been retold in plays and poems and songs, although the story is always different—the Wandering Jew is old, or young, or he grows old and is reborn a young man. He can even be a woman, Salome or the Queen of Sheba. He can be good, although usually he's feared and blamed for bringing misery to everyone he meets."

Mona does not respond. Sometimes she enjoys Moses's stories, sometimes she doesn't. They are like stories her father told, reminders of her childhood days, and that she enjoys, but Moses is apt to tell stories when he wants to be evasive, and that is what he is doing now.

"Everyone in the world seems to be out enjoying the sunshine," he says. "If I ever move back to North City this is the neighborhood where I'll live." He cranes his neck to peer up at the narrow Victorians hovering, like nervous men, over the sidewalks.

"Are you planning to move back soon, dear?"

"You never can tell."

"You know, when we first moved to the valley, I made Izzy promise that it would be temporary." She and Izzy came to North City from New York right after they were married. "I was a kid, I loved the spectacular views, the nightclubs, the excitement. I loved my job in the travel agency. I was a file clerk and I got to read all the travel brochures. But Izzy hated the congestion. He longed for chaparral and coyotes, and somewhere along the way I guess we both forgot his promise to me because I got converted."

"I never have. Look at these houses! Every shade of the rainbow."

Mona stares up at a rising sun carved under the eaves of a rickety wooden house across the street.

"And the traffic. Listen." They stop walking. "Doesn't it sound like the ocean roaring?"

Mona laughs.

"And the people, all kinds of people—there, the Black girl on her bike, those two old Mexican men walking so slowly, the red-headed guy with the scarf wound around his neck, the Lesbian lovers holding hands. Everyone's here. The bay spreads out its arms, inviting them to come. The old-timers, the new arrivals who give the neighborhood meaning. Did you see the apartment house we passed a while back? Apartmentos de la Esperanza—apartments of hope. This is the beginning. Orchard Valley is the end, a fence of mountains cutting off the air supply. The ground underfoot is warm and spongy and if you don't watch out you sink in and then there is no way to get the leverage you need to pull yourself out." He throws up his hands. "Oh, lord. Thank you for the wind and the salt air and the smell of sulfur. And thank you for the Shell station, for Marcelo's bar, for Century Rugs and Carpets and the Baptist church. And thank you for the Catholic church too, and the Dim Sum parlor, and the Salvador movie theater, and the African Art Gallery, and gutters festooned with styrofoam cups and beer cans, and apartments growing out of the tops of stores." He turns to Mona. "I have an enormous longing to live here."

"I never knew you didn't like the valley. I mean, I know you've only lived there three years, but I assumed you liked it because you never said you didn't. Your whole life is there."

"My work is there."

"And so am I," she says nervously.

He smiles down on her. "And so are you." He takes her hand.

20

Jasmine Village,
Monday evening, December 8

WIND TEARS LEAVES from the trees, dropping them down to cling to the sides of cars like tiny hands. Adina and Mona run from the parking lot into the Trains and Things Toy Shop. While Mona takes refuge in the back, Adina pushes through the crowded store, heading straight for the game counter to buy Trivial Pursuit for Gideon, and here, where toys radiate colored light, she meets her friends Caroline Algren and Portia Twohy.

"What's wrong?" Adina asks. It is immediately apparent from the women's expressions that something has happened.

"The Kennedys were robbed. It happened an hour ago," Portia whispers.

"The Kennedys?" Adina murmurs. Tom is an old schoolmate of Gideon's and all three women know Louise. It is difficult to believe that someone she knows could be robbed. The women draw close together.

"Louise was picking up Nina and Natasha at dancing class," Caroline says.

Portia says the robbers took jewelry, money, appliances, everything—even wrapped-up Christmas presents. They seemed to know when the house would be empty, left it a mess.

Adina stands in silence. She recalls the conversations Mona overheard at work. The men mentioned Bonanza Way, where the Kennedys live, and Adina is shaken by this coincidence because Gideon has told her more than once that he is convinced Mona imagined the conversations, any talk about a robbery on Bonanza Way was sheer fantasy. He was furious when he heard Mona had been to see the sheriff, said they must think she's crazy.

"I can't imagine what happened," Portia is saying and Caroline is nodding in agreement.

"It can't be anyone from Lexington, not with the roads patrolled," Caroline whispers.

"But then who can it be? Maybe they got through the patrol," Portia says.

Adina sadly shakes her head. Maybe Portia is right. Maybe the robbers somehow got past the patrol. Gideon has said more than once that a robber or a kidnapper was bound to steal over the hills from Lexington some night. They all have dark skin and no one would see. He said that was why it was important to build the new jail, to set an example, to frighten the criminals away. For herself, Adina does not know what to think. She wishes Mona had never mentioned Shoemaker or Bonanza Way.

Mona stands among children dressed in denims and T-shirts, watching a yellow electric train speeding around a silver track. She and the children are motionless, still photos; only the train moves, over bridges, through mountains, its coal car spilling real coal, the engineer wearing real denim overalls and waving a real American flag.

A doll displayed on a table catches Mona's attention. A large orange tag identifies him as Topper. She loves his raggedy coat and pointed black hat with a turned-up brim, his skinny wrinkled body hunched over a walking stick. "Is this a new movie star we've missed hearing about?" Mona asks a little girl who also seems intrigued.

The girl smiles shyly and shakes her head.

"He's sort of nifty, don't you think? I mean after you get used to him he's actually cute."

She smiles again. "I'd love to have him for Christmas."

"Well, maybe Santa Claus will be obliging." They stare reverently at Topper and then Mona says, "He looks like he's returning from a long hike. Maybe he was in Sonora panning for gold."

"On the way home he had to walk through a forest where a vampire drank all his blood," the girl says.

Mona is startled to hear such an ugly thought coming from such a pretty girl. "He got away though," she hastens to add. "That's important to remember. He got away."

"Batman saved him."

"Batman? Well, I guess maybe it was Batman. He touched his magic button and Batman suddenly appeared. See it there— the little gold circle pinned onto his shirt? It's a magic pin."

"His son ran away from home. He's looking for his son," the child says. "See that spot on his forehead. It won't come off until he finds his son."

Mona had not noticed the spot before. "Maybe it's a cinder."

"It's blood. That's where the vampire sucked blood," the child says, and now Mona does not answer because this child's obsession with vampires is unnerving and she finds she does not like the doll.

She backs away, turns and sees Adina and her friends talking at the front of the store, looking so somber, their long shadows crisscrossing the floor. She asks Adina what is wrong. Adina whispers the story. Mona nods. She can hear Shoemaker's words, see the vandalized trees. The prophecy is fulfilled, but now is not the time to say it.

As Portia and Caroline talk quietly, Mona and Adina stand side by side, neither saying what is on her mind.

21

Mona's cottage,
an hour later

"EVERYONE WAS terribly upset," Mona says. She is in front of the TV, video on, audio off, bag of potato chips in her lap, holding the telephone receiver between her shoulder and ear.

"Did Adina make the connection? I mean, you've told her, haven't you, about what we heard Shoemaker say?" Dorothy asks from the other end.

"Oh, I've told her. I don't know, though, if she's made any connections. She has a way, you know, of seeing what she wants to see—"

"Tell me."

"I decided not to say anything to her tonight, she looked so disturbed."

"I think you're right. Wait until she's calmer. Well, well, isn't this something."

"It's coming true. Like a bad dream."

"It sure enough is."

"They'll believe us now, don't you think? The sheriff I mean."

"Honey, what the sheriff's going to do I do not know. I have no thoughts on that subject. You'll understand what I'm saying when I tell you my news."

"Your news?"

"Yes. Joe Bourne called Leon—"

"What did he find out?"

"Shoemaker's not in jail in Cincinnati."

"He's not? Are you sure?"

"That's what Joe said."

"Was he in jail? A few days ago?"

"No. And Joe couldn't find him in jail anyplace else."

"Then Malmquist's supervisor was lying?"

"Your guess is as good as mine, Mona. Could be the supervisor is lying. Could be the Cincinnati police gave out the wrong information."

The supervisor is lying, Mona is sure. He is involved with Shoemaker. That is what Leon thinks. It is what Sam thinks, and Mona herself certainly has heard enough about police corruption on TV. Still, though, it is hard to believe. "Dorothy, what if I talk to Mayor Hambly? His son Tommy was in school with Adina for a while, so he knows me, and maybe he can find out what's going on, with the sheriff, you know."

"Good idea, Mona."

"Perhaps you should come along. I think you two probably have something in common. I mean, Hambly has opposed development in the valley, hasn't he?"

"You bet he has, honey. He opposed the scheme to combine Jasmine and Rancho into a city."

"So he's probably sympathetic to what you're trying to do in Lexington, and that might make him take me seriously."

"Okay, if you're sure you want me along."

"I'm sure." Mona hears a rustling sound outside. Someone is walking on dry leaves, and quickly she tells Dorothy goodbye, runs to the door, around to the side of the cottage—no one is there. Slowly she retraces her steps, telling herself she is hearing things because she is jittery. She turns the corner to the front of her cottage where she sees a small dark shadow dart out from behind one of the madrones, then disappear behind another. It is some small animal, a raccoon or maybe a cat. "Zebadiah, is that you? Kitty, kitty? Are you back?"

22

TOWN HALL IS a late nineteenth-century Victorian mansion set in what is now a small park, a rose garden on the edge of Jasmine Village, where even in December roses are still in bloom.

Dorothy says, "Those ripply gray shingles look like a Louis-the-Fifteenth wig, and the two round windows are the eyes of Louis himself glowering at everyone who passes by."

Mona stares up at the building in amusement.

In all the years she has lived in Jasmine, she has never been inside Town Hall. As they walk across the huge foyer, she is awed by the enormous oak fireplace and the endless display of Persian rugs.

Dorothy glances at the pictures on the walls of Jasmine officials past and present. "Not going to find my Uncle Caspar among those stern white men.... Won't find your relatives there either, Mona."

Mona knows that not many Jews have ever lived in Jasmine. She and Izzy discussed this before they moved from North City, and after they moved they sometimes were snubbed by people who thought they looked like foreigners and who made fun of the way they talked. But there were friendly neighbors too, and over the years Mona thought less and less about being Jewish.

Curtis Hambly, a short man with a round face, comes out of his office to warmly invite the women in as if he is inviting them into his home. He asks after Adina, "and how's her family—two boys is it?" and Mona asks after his son. "Tommy's a lawyer in Portland now," he tells her. "I can hardly believe it," she replies. "I think the last time I saw him his voice must have been five octaves higher than it is now."

"And you, Mrs. Michael? Have we met? Your name's familiar."

"Dorothy's the author of three published mystery novels and president of Black Women United in Lexington—"

"Ah, of course. I've read about Black Women United in the *Herald*. You must know I support your effort one hundred percent. We've had our struggles here with the same developers. I think they finally got the message that we meant 'no.' I must say I'm sorry to see them trying to get a foothold in Lexington."

"Well, I want you to understand that we mean 'no,' Mayor Hambly, and I'll let you in on a secret. I think we're going to win."

Hambly smiles. "Now, let's see, your council is due to vote this week, isn't it?"

"They were supposed to vote this week, but now they've postponed the vote, scheduled it for next week, you know, closer to Christmas. I'm sure they hope that no one from the community will attend the meeting."

Hambly nods.

"I think they're in for a surprise though. We've mailed out five thousand informational flyers. Council members have already started getting phone calls, and to tell you the truth I think a few of them are getting a little scared because they're trying to stall even more, trying to postpone the vote until next year, although I think that tactic is going to backfire too because it gives us more time for publicity. They're hoping tempers will simmer down over the holidays and people will forget. What they haven't considered is that they've given us time to mount a media campaign."

Dorothy is about to fill Hambly in on the gossip about individual council members, but he interrupts to say, "Well, I wish you the best," and he pushes a button on his desk, which brings a woman he calls Mary to the door. He asks Mary to bring coffee then turns back to Mona and Dorothy and says, "Now, what can I do for you ladies?"

23

MONA HAS HELEN and Shirley in the sunroom crocheting toy pandas for Christmas presents, working slowly with knobby hands. Hanks of bright wool lie on an end table, and Mona sings "All I Want for Christmas is My Two Front Teeth," as the older women hum softly along. Lil is behind them in her wheel-chair, eyes closed.

Maryalice appears suddenly in the doorway. "Oh, you came out of nowhere. You took me by surprise," Mona says. She stares at Maryalice for a moment because she has never seen her looking so radiant.

Helen is about to begin a paw and is having trouble break-ing off the red yarn and attaching yellow. Mona does it for her.

Maryalice walks into the room. "It's too hard for her," she says. "You get them frustrated and then they lose their confidence."

"Helen can't tie knots but she can do everything else," Mona counters.

Colleen hurries in with medicine for Shirley. "Heard about the robbery in Jasmine?" she asks no one in particular as she hands Shirley a glass of water.

"Yes, the Kennedys. It's very upsetting," Mona answers.

"Louise and Tom Kennedy? Oh, the robbery on Tuesday. I'm talking about today, this morning, just now, a couple hours ago, the Lewises."

Mona drops the yarn. "Which Lewises?"

"Ned and Emmy Lou. Do you know them? They live on Mother Lode Lane in Victor's Grove."

Mona nods. She has known Ned Lewis's father Dave for years.

"Mrs. Lewis was taking the kids to school," Lucy says. "Everyone thinks the robbers were waiting outside and broke in as soon as they saw her drive away. I mean, she wasn't gone for very long. How long does it take to run the kids to school? But, boy, when she got back the house was a shambles, stuff all over. They even took the Christmas presents."

Maryalice slips across the room to stand behind Lil's wheelchair as Colleen continues with her story. Mona is fascinated to see Maryalice smiling all the while Colleen relates the bad news. Clearly she is not listening, she has something more important on her mind. Her face is so red she could be blushing. She must be in love, or maybe she is just horny.

"Glad I don't live in Victor's Grove. Two robberies in two days," Colleen says.

"Yes, two robberies." Mona returns her attention to Colleen. "Two robberies and the trees."

"The trees?" Maryalice says disdainfully.

"The trees that were vandalized on Bonanza Way. I don't think that's ever happened before either, not in Jasmine."

"She's right, you know," Colleen says to Maryalice. "There's something sadistic about these robberies—I mean it feels to me like they're trying to frighten people as much as take their money. I can't explain why, but that's how it feels." She takes the glass from Shirley and leaves the room.

"I doubt that robbers would bother to vandalize trees," Maryalice murmurs, then turning to Lil she says, "You'll come with me, Mrs. Sternberg. Nurse Whipple has to do some tests." She pulls Lil away from the circle, away from Mona, but Lil reacts at once, pushing down on the brake lever, causing the wheelchair to jerk to a halt. "Watch out for Maryalice. She hates Jews," she says loudly. Her voice is gravelly and moist.

"It's okay, dear," Mona whispers. "I'll still be here when you're through."

"Uncle Gabe says Maryalice isn't in love."

"Isn't in love? How did—" How did Lil know Mona was thinking Maryalice was in love, and how did she know about Uncle Gabe? Has Mona mentioned him to her? For the life of her she cannot remember. She is about to ask but never does because Maryalice, clearly insulted by Lil's comment, pushes suddenly on Lil's wheelchair, opening the brake.

As she wheels Lil away, Lil calls back to Mona, "Maryalice isn't in love. She's glowing because she's digesting the blood of her latest victim."

 24

Sam's kitchen,
an hour later

"THERE'S BEEN another robbery!"

"I know."

"You know?"

"Uh huh. Carlos told me. He heard a customer talking about it. The Lewises of Mother Lode Lane in Victor's Grove. Every-

thing we heard your friend Mr. Shoemaker say is coming true."
Dorothy grins.

Mona smiles sheepishly. "This is terrible, Dorothy. I mean here I am happy that Ned's been robbed, enjoying someone else's misery."

"Honey, you're not enjoying someone else's misery. You're feeling good because you've been vindicated. Nothing wrong with that, but Mona, don't count on Malmquist's supervisor believing you. Don't set your hopes too high. Sometimes people don't want to listen to you because of who you are and they aren't necessarily going to believe you because you're right. Possibly Mayor Hambly will, although I wouldn't count on him either."

"He was so friendly—"

"He was pleasant enough, but that's the way politicians are. They're sweet as syrup and tell you they'll help, which only means that the secretary will put in a call to some official: 'Mr. Hambly is sorry to be such a bother. He was hoping you could give him something to tell these women to get them off his back.' Happens all the time." She bends over to pull a tray of croissants out of the oven.

"Maybe I should call Deputy Malmquist's supervisor then, not wait for Hambly."

"I don't think that'll do any good. If Hambly puts the screws on the sheriff, the sheriff'll do something. Otherwise, whatever the reasons, I don't think those men are interested in Shoemaker. We're probably going to have to consider ways to warn people ourselves—"

"What do you mean, dear, warn people ourselves?"

"Get the word out, capture people's attention. Set a fire under the sheriff."

"Set a fire? Oh, Dorothy, I think I've gone about as far as I can." Aren't the police supposed to track down Shoemaker, find him and lock him up, let her get back to her life, and isn't the press supposed to get the word out? What does she know about P.R.? She is making a spectacle of herself as it is and no one believes her—not Malmquist's supervisor, not Adina, not Moses. Dorothy, this is going too far, she is about to say, but the words stick to her tongue. She hears a voice calling to her from behind the refrigerator. "I know it's you, Uncle Gabe," she grumbles. "I've done all I'm going to do, so you're wasting your time." How she wishes everyone—Shoemaker, Malmquist, Malmquist's supervisor, Maryalice, Uncle Gabe—everyone would leave her alone. To her relief the voice fades. It is suddenly so quiet she can hear the sound of the gas fire in the oven and then, oddly, the echo of her own voice telling Dorothy, "Maybe we should call Ren Davis."

"Ren who? I can't hear you," Dorothy replies. She is bent over, has her head in the oven.

"Ren Davis. He's mayor of Rancho."

"Oh, sure, I've heard of him."

"He must know that sooner or later whatever happens in Jasmine is going to affect Rancho." Not waiting for Dorothy's reply, Mona hurries down the back hall to the pay phone to leave an urgent message for Davis. His secretary says he is in a meeting.

Back in the kitchen, she finds Sam standing in the doorway watching Dorothy cutting dough. "Hi, Sam. You look like an intern watching a master surgeon performing a quadruple bypass."

He laughs. "Hear about the robbery?"

"Carlos has spread the word," Dorothy replies.

"Yeah, we've heard all about it," Mona says.

"Strange, huh?" Sam murmurs. "Two incidents so close to-gether."

"Three," Mona says.

"Three it is," Dorothy agrees. "The Kennedys, the Lewises, and the trees."

"What trees?"

"The ones they vandalized on Bonanza Way."

He shrugs. "I'd thought that was kids, but you could be right. These guys sure seem to be trying to scare the shit out of people. I hadn't heard about the Lewises. Too bad."

Dorothy looks up. "Then which robberies are you talking about?"

"The Kennedys, over on Bonanza Way—"

"Yeah."

"And Al Dixon."

"Who's he?"

Sam frowns. "I don't know who he is. He's a guy. Lives in Victor's Grove."

"And he got robbed today?" Dorothy asks.

"Yeah, a couple hours ago. He and his wife left for work, and when the cleaning woman came in later she found the place a mess. It's sort of ironic. I know Al's brother and he says Al's living way beyond his means, used to live in Lexing-ton, got up to his eyebrows in debt to move into the valley to get away from crime."

SHE DECIDES SHE will stop at the Lewis's to offer sympathy.

She tried Mayor Davis again, but his secretary said he was still in a meeting. She explained that her message was urgent, it concerned the robberies in Jasmine, and the secretary finally agreed to interrupt him, but then Mona's quarter ran out and by the time she had rummaged through her purse and found another quarter it was one minute past five and when she called back she was greeted by an answering machine. She cannot get through to Davis, Curtis Hambly hasn't called, and two robberies today in Victor's Grove. Too much is happening too quickly.

She turns onto Bonanza Way and then left onto Mother Lode Lane. A crowd is gathered outside the Lewis's house and her first thought is that the robbers have returned to take what they left behind, since she has heard many times on TV that this is what robbers do—they are in a hurry, or their sacks are too small, and they return to finish the job, and then they return again after the victims have had time to replace the stolen valuables. She parks across the road. Although it is too dark to make out people's faces, Emmy Lou is clearly visible in the brightly lit doorway, framed on either side by low-growing trees which look like shaggy soldiers marching towards her. A television van labeled Channel Fifty-Three, the local cable channel, is parked in the driveway, and a cameraman is threading his way to the front door.

Mona joins the crowd, tells the young man standing next to her, "I never realized it required so much equipment, for one interview, you know. Isn't this awful what's happening?

When I saw all these people I was afraid there'd been another robbery. I'm so relieved."

He asks her if she lives nearby and she tells him, "Yes. I'm just over the hill, on Madrone Road. Oh, dear. You don't think I'll be next, do you?"

He asks if she has lived in Jasmine long, and she replies, "Forty years," but her voice is hesitant now because she wonders why he is asking so many questions. She is suddenly aware that this man is lanky and blond, and she squints for a closer look at his face. His features are lost in the shadows. This is not Shoemaker, she reassures herself, and he seems to read her mind—or did he hear her? He extends his hand, tells her he is Todd Erikson, a reporter with Channel Fifty-Three, here to cover the story, which is of interest because there is so little crime in the valley. He asks if she has heard or seen anything suspicious, anything at all.

26

Veronica Crabbe's,
Friday evening, December 12

THE WAITRESS BRINGS a cauldron of cioppino and a huge basket of sourdough bread and three bibs, blue for Gideon, pink for Mona and Adina. Veronica Crabbe's is a converted riverboat. Thick redwood pillars stand guard in the main dining room while dark portholes stare in from the river and music hovers overhead.

Mona and Adina giggle as Gideon struggles to tie on his bib, then talk softly about the boys until Gideon wipes his mouth and says to Mona, "I hear you were on TV last night."

She *was* on TV, on the eleven o'clock news, answering Todd Erikson's questions with surprising authority. Several neighbors called to say they had seen her. Carlos called too, and Debbie, the secretary at the convalescent home. Mona was startled and pleased by the attention.

The interview was rerun on the Channel Fifty-Three morning news, and then at noon she and Sam and Dorothy watched Sheriff Salwen's rebuttal in front of the County Building in Orchard Hills. Salwen, tall and double-jointed, sounding something like Chester from Gunsmoke, said he was working around the clock to apprehend the burglars. He said he was aware of Mrs. Pinsky's theories but her facts didn't check out and it would be better if she returned to her TV movies and left policing to the police. Dorothy was furious. She snapped off the TV, said Salwen was trying to make Mona look like a fool. Sam turned it back on just as the reporter was signing off and the camera was panning across Overlook Hill behind the Hall of Justice, the proposed site for the new county jail. After that, no one called.

The annoyance in Gideon's voice is unmistakable and out of habit Mona begins to say, I know I looked silly, but the words never take form. She considers telling Gideon that something sinister is going on right under their noses and it is her duty to let people know, but these words are uncomfortable too, and so she remains silent, taking the loaf of bread firmly in both hands, yanking off a chunk, dipping it into the soup.

Gideon is obviously furious.

Adina stares down at crab claws swimming in the cauldron. She cannot bear to watch this silent battle. She wishes her mother had never laid eyes on John Shoemaker. Now that she has, why can't she see how her nosiness makes Gideon feel? Why can't she forget the whole thing? Why can't the county stop procrastinating and hire Gideon to design the new jail? "We missed your interview, Mom," she says, trying to make peace. "Gideon got home from work at ten and we went right to bed."

Gideon swallows and says to Mona, "I didn't see you. I heard all about it though, and today I saw Mayor Hambly."

"Mayor Hambly?" Mona did not realize he was on TV.

"Well, it's not so awful, Gideon. Mom's just trying to get the word out." Adina turns to Mona and says, "Mom, it's hard on Gideon having you go over the sheriff's head to the press and the mayor, especially now in the middle of negotiations with the board of supervisors." Her eyes dart quickly back to Gideon, as if she is trying to build a bridge between him and her mother.

"What did Hambly say?" Mona asks.

"He said you were a well-meaning senior citizen," Gideon tells her.

"Oh, he did not, Mom," Adina breaks in. "He just said he thought you were well meaning but the sheriff was doing a good job—"

"You saw Hambly too?"

Adina nods and says desperately, "Gideon's about to present his final sketches for the jail—here, Love, let me show them to Mom." She reaches for Gideon's attaché case.

"You saw Hambly's interview? Why didn't you say anything in the car?" She and Adina met Gideon at the restaurant, drove all the way to Veronica Crabbe's alone together, yet Adina did not say a thing. This is more upsetting to Mona than the robberies.

"We were rushed. You were late getting home, Mom....
Come on, let's forget about that, okay?"

Let's forget? Mona stares at Adina. There has never been
this sort of dishonesty between them before.

Adina unzips the attaché case, carefully pulling out a sheet
of onionskin that she lays on the table. "Imagine the view from
the top of Hyde Street, the whole valley, okay?"

Mona sighs. Maybe they can talk later, after they get home.
She glances down at Gideon's sketches.

"Imagine a view of the whole valley, almost three hundred
sixty degrees, the hills, the towns. And imagine being in Jasmine Village, coming home from shopping, looking up, far in
the distance."

The drawing is of a square brick building, each brick me-
ticulously pencilled in, and two stories of landscaped terraces.
"It's gorgeous," Mona says without much enthusiasm. "I love
the steps running from the street up to the little room at the
top. They look something like snakes."

"That's not a room. It's the guard tower," Gideon grumbles.

"Mom, it's a modern version of the Tower of Babel. Isn't it
wonderful? Isn't it timeless?"

Mona nods. It's a weird-looking thing, she thinks, but if the
county buys it, that's all that matters.

"Gideon has designed it so it can be added onto. He's
worked up a five-tiered tower, just in case there's a lot of business." Adina laughs. "Walt likes it a lot and says Gideon's definitely front-runner—so anyway, Mom, Gideon wishes you'd
cool it."

"Cool it?" Mona is not sure what Adina means. Gideon has
fished a crab claw from the cauldron and somehow he manages to keep his expression calm and businesslike as he sucks
out the juice, although Mona can tell that he is really quite

nervous because he is bouncing his knee up and down and the table is wobbling.

"Yes, cool it." Her mother does not seem to get the point of this conversation and Adina is growing impatient. "Now's not the time to make waves."

"But what about the robbers, Adina? This very minute they could be robbing someone's house. We know who they are and someone has to apprehend them."

Adina shakes her head. "Let someone else worry about the robbers."

Mona would be happy to let someone else worry about the robbers, but no one seems interested. She would like to give in to Adina's demand, but she knows that if she did Uncle Gabe's voice would buzz in her ear. She wants desperately to please Adina but does not know how.

27

Later that night

SHE DREAMS THAT she and her family are at the dining room table eating burritos when a stranger climbs in through the window, asking if he may join the party. The stranger is a middle-aged man dressed in a monk's hat and a blood-red coat; a yellow beard coils around his body. He circles the room, leaving a line of footprints behind him.

He is old. He circles the room. He is young. He is dressed in a black coat and yellow pantaloons. A spidery red mark is etched on his forehead. Adina hands him a bowl of soup. He shaves off his beard with a holly leaf. Under the chandelier, his body casts no shadow.

Please sit, Mona tells him. He replies that he cannot sit still because of some neurosis he inherited from his Jewish grandmother. He takes two steps backward and three steps forward, backward, forward. His feet wear a hole in the soft pine floor.

He drops into the hole. Soldiers shoot him with long thin rifles. Bullets ricochet off his body and soar into the sky. A wild boar jumps down from a tree to eat him. He crawls through its belly and out its eye, while Mona and Adina and Gideon and Andrew and Ian play musical chairs to "Silent Night."

When the music stops, Mona sits and Gideon butts her off the chair.

Adobe Reservoir Park,
Saturday, December 13

THE ROAD TWISTS for miles along the border separating Lexington from Orchard Valley. It ends at the park, at a point overlooking the reservoir, where the sun's pale reflection stares up from the water. Mona and Moses take blankets from the car trunk and claim a sheltered spot on the deserted beach.

Mona, still shaken by the TV interview, the attention, the rejection, especially Gideon's rejection, tries to find a bright side to share. "It's strange," she says, "seeing yourself on the screen with bulges and wrinkles you never admitted you had. It's funny, because you like the woman you're watching too."

Moses replies, "I didn't catch the newscast, although I certainly heard about it." He grins. "Shirley was beside herself seeing you a star and, if you can believe it, Helen was actually laughing."

"I wish my kids had such positive feelings." She tells him a little about their reaction.

"But you can understand, can't you? They're frightened, and when people are frightened they...they lash out at whoever's close at hand.... And you have to realize too that a lot of people aren't going to want to believe you. It's not only Gideon and Adina. They want to feel safe, and here you are trying to tell them that sinister people may be in their midst— not Blacks from Lexington, not people who are easy to identify, but white businessmen just like them. They have to believe you're altogether wrong because you're upsetting their sense of safety, you see."

"Yes, I know. A lot of people don't like to think about unpleasant things." Moses is one of them, and Mona has to admit that sometimes so is she. "But don't you see, dear, what infuriates me is that the robberies could be prevented if Salwen simply asked the newspapers and TV stations to run Shoemaker's picture." She desperately wants him to understand. Why can't you let yourself take me seriously, share my outrage? If you really loved me.... That is what the voice within her would have her say. She stifles it, telling herself now isn't the time.

"Why would he publicize Shoemaker's picture if he's convinced the man's in jail?" Moses pulls off his sneakers and rolls up his pants. He walks out towards the water, far out, until watery footprints are following him.

I'm talking to myself, Mona mutters. "I talk to myself when I'm alone and I talk to myself when I'm with you," she calls after him. Does he hear? To the west, water splashes gently against sharp rocks; from the east come faint barking noises that break the silence. Must be seals, she thinks. They've left the ocean, come across dry land to this spot to protect me. "I think Zebadiah isn't dead after all," she calls out. She rolls up her pants, trudges out towards the water, and when she is at his side she tells him about the shadowy animal she saw the other night. "I'm almost sure it was a cat. I thought I saw a crimp at the end of its tail, like Zebadiah's. I left the window open and a bowl of food. Last night when I got home from work the food was gone."

Moses looks at her absently. "Sounds to me like Zebadiah's returned."

"I wonder why he left. I had him fixed."

"Maybe it isn't sex. Maybe he simply wants to remain a free spirit, you see, not to be tied down to a house or person but to roam free the way God intended." There is a disquieting edge to Moses's voice, and Mona's discomfort intensifies when he kneels down and frantically scoops up a pile of sand.

"Building a castle?" she asks helplessly.

He nods.

She picks small reddish stones off the sand, tosses them into the water—burnt offerings, she says. "Your castle looks suspiciously like the convalescent home, dear."

He sits back on his haunches and examines his work. "You're right." He scratches a cobblestone path around the structure. "How's that?"

"Lovely."

He grins.

"Maryalice and I had another run-in," she tells him.

"Yes, I know."

"She told you?"

He nods.

"I didn't realize she confided things like that in you. Does she often confide in you?"

He shrugs.

"What did she tell you?"

He does not answer immediately. "She thinks you take too much responsibility, considering you're only a volunteer," he finally says.

"And what did you say?"

"I don't know. I guess I said something to the effect that I thought you were competent, you were more effective than some of the social workers."

"It sounds like you don't want to talk about it."

"I don't mind. It's not important though. She's under pressure, says things she doesn't mean."

"Like what?"

"She said Debbie needed help in the office with Medi-Cal forms—"

"What does that have to do with me?... You don't mean Maryalice expects me to do the Medi-Cal forms?"

"I told her I didn't think you knew how to type."

"What's going on, Moses?"

He avoids her eyes, smooths the sides of his castle.

"What's going on?" she repeats.

"I've taken the job at the Esperanza Convalescent Home," he says softly. "I begin on the fifth."

"You've taken a job in North City?" she whispers.

He nods. "Maryalice will replace me here. The board will announce it next week."

"You're going to commute every day?"

"I found a small apartment—"

"You're moving to North City? You never said anything?" Her voice is suddenly loud.

He scoops up another pile of sand and begins constructing another nursing home castle. "I didn't want to tell you until I was sure—I knew you'd be upset." He looks timidly at Mona. "Nothing's changing, sweetie. We can still get together on weekends. Maybe not quite so often, but haven't we always agreed to hang loose? It'll be just the same between us, you'll see."

Indian Mountain State Park,
Sunday afternoon, December 14

MONA SUSPECTS ANDREW has read every issue of *National Geographic* ever published. He knows that chaparral is Spanish for low-growing bush, that the chaps cowboys wear on their legs come from the same word, that creosote bushes exude some sort of poison so that other plants won't grow nearby and steal their water. She and Ian and Andrew are a hundred yards below the crest of Indian Mountain. Clouds swirl in and out of shallow caves. Andrew says that most of the Indians after whom Indian Mountain was named died of smallpox they caught from white settlers. He has heard that their spirits live in the rocks.

Mona is still trying to absorb Moses's announcement. She could not sleep and spent most of the night watching TV. This morning she was so depressed and exhausted she wanted to cancel the outing with the boys, but then Uncle Gabe appeared and made a fuss and she decided a change of scenery might do her good.

The boys unstrap their seat belts and bolt out of the car and down a narrow trail. Soon they are high above the parking lot where Ian swings from the limb of an ancient oak, while Andrew, wearing a bright red sweat suit, scurries up the rocks like a crab.

Andrew finds an oyster shell trapped in the surface of a sandstone boulder, a huge rock that sometime long ago broke away from the mountain. "Did you know that Indian Mountain's been under water three times, Grandma?" he calls out.

"Yes, I knew, dear—watch out for the stones!"

"I'm okay—do you know where those holes come from?" He is pointing at a large slab of sandstone, which is smooth except for three small holes.

"That's where the Indians ground acorns."

"How did you know that, Grandma?"

"Oh, I know all sorts of things. The Indians used acorns to make bread. They boiled the meal first to get rid of the bitter taste."

Andrew stares at her with dark eyes—Mona's eyes. "Grandma, look at the deer, two of them!"

She turns to see two brown streaks disappearing behind a clump of bushes, and off to the right is a man sitting on a rock, surrounded by wisps of fog. She cannot make out his features, is overcome with a sense of fear because he seems to be tall and thin, like Shoemaker, although he is wearing a strange wide-brimmed hat. She reaches into her purse for her distance glasses. She cannot tell. Perhaps she could see more clearly if she were looking down on him, if she climbed up the trail. But what is she thinking of when the children are with her? He could easily follow and there would be no escape. She tells herself she is dreaming nonsense because the man probably bears no resemblance to Shoemaker at all, although it is possible that Shoemaker would follow her after seeing her on TV.... "It's getting chilly, boys. Let's go back to the car and go to the Indian museum instead."

"Aw, we just got here, Grandma," Ian calls down from a high limb. But he slips down without further argument—perhaps he catches the urgency in her voice. He and Andrew dart out of sight around a bend, heading back towards the parking lot, and she follows as fast as she can. "Don't get too far ahead of me!"

They wait for her to catch her breath, surrounded by sandstone formations scarred by moss and lichens, green graffiti. Behind them, the man comes, fog swirling around him. She walks quickly ahead, motioning for the boys to follow. "Kids, I'm a magician and I've just waved my wand. It's five thousand B.C. and we're cave dwellers, the only people for thousands of miles, and we're hunting for dinosaurs." She is running now. Where she gets the speed she never knows. She races down the trail, twisting and turning until she sees a cave that is a little deeper than the rest. She leads the way inside, and the three of them wait on their hands and knees in darkness. "Ssshh." She puts her finger over her lips. Sharp stones on the cave floor cut into their hands and knees, but they remain huddled together as the man flashes by.

"That was the dinosaur," she whispers. "Dinosaurs shoot fire out of their nostrils when they're provoked."

"That's what dragons do, not dinosaurs," Andrew insists. "Besides, dinosaurs were already fossils when cave dwellers lived."

She tells him details aren't important so long as they make a beeline to the car. The parking area is directly below them and they leave the path, groping their way down steep rocks, sliding as the rocks disintegrate into gravel. Mona falls and skins her knee. She picks herself up and continues. They drive through the northern gate. She floors the accelerator, even on hairpin turns, until she is absolutely certain they are not being followed.

Outside the park, the sun shines over a cluster of ranch houses bearing the sign Executive Community. "Did you guys know that forty years ago, when Grandpa and I first moved to Jasmine, this was a horse ranch?"

Andrew nods his head.

"Why was the man chasing us, Grandma?" Ian asks.

"What man?"

"The man you said was the dinosaur," Andrew answers.

"Oh, I don't think he was chasing us. I think he was taking a walk. I was fooling, sweetheart." She hopes that satisfies them. The last thing she needs is for Adina to find out what happened. "Look, boys, horses in the yard over there," she says cheerfully.

"There used to be more horses in Orchard County than anywhere else in the United States, except Kentucky," Andrew replies. "Did you know that, Grandma?"

SOMETHING IS WRONG. The lights were off when she left, Mona is certain. But now from the road the windows of her cottage are yellow against a darkening sky. Has Shoemaker invaded her home? She musters all the self-control she can as she pulls slowly into the driveway, pats the boys casually on their backsides, and says, "Hurry now. It's almost dinner time." She watches them dash across the lawn and disappear into their kitchen before she leaves her car.

It is worse than she imagined. Adina is righting the drop-leaf table, which is overturned in the middle of the room. The pictures of Izzy and Great Uncle Gabe are smashed. Slivers of glass lie in chaotic patterns on the rug.

"What happened?" Mona whispers.

"I don't know what happened," Adina says. "We saw the lights on but your car wasn't here. We just walked in this minute."

"They made a mess. That's what happened," Gideon says, emerging from the bathroom. Forks and spoons and cracker boxes and soup cans have been torn out of drawers and cupboards. The freezer door is open and TV dinners and frozen orange juice cans are strewn about the floor.

This is Shoemaker's work, Mona is certain. His long body has been in her cottage, his long fingers have touched everything in sight.

She stares into the blank TV screen, expecting to find his face buried inside, the broad mouth, the deep-set eyes, but now it occurs to her that the TV set is where she left it this morning and that is strange. She runs to the closet to check her jewelry box. "My jewelry's all here!" The box is stuffed, as it was this morning, with all her precious possessions—capricorn earrings, Indian beads, Grandmother Burkholtz's lapis lazuli ring. "The toaster's here too," in its proper place on the kitchen counter, and the microwave oven, and the Mr. Coffee machine. "They didn't take anything," she says aloud.

"Then why were they here?" Adina whispers.

"Look in the bathroom, if you want to know why," Gideon says harshly.

"The bathroom too?" What could they possibly want in the bathroom? Were they looking for drugs? Mona is breathless. The bathroom door is wide open, and, "Oh!"—the mirror. Toothpaste is smeared on the mirror.... Someone has drawn a toothpaste picture, a pig, fat, huge tits dragging on the ground, a ring in its nose, a curly tail.

"That's gross," Adina gasps.

A woman, a stick-figure woman, suckles the pig, and toothpaste swastikas framing the picture cut Mona's image into cubist segments.

"They didn't come here to take anything, Mona," Gideon says. "They were here to warn little old ladies to mind their own business. Why can't you take advice for a change?" His pale eyes glare from behind her in the mirror.

"But they vandalized my house, Gideon! Why are you mad at *me*?"

"Gideon's not mad at you, Mom." Adina's voice is shaking. "It's just very upsetting having this happen when life is complicated enough. I mean, now you'll have to report to the police again." She realizes she is angry. Why can't her mother stay out of the spotlight? Why can't she see that this is the last thing Gideon needs, with the contract not yet settled? Why can't she see that none of this would have happened if she hadn't made such a fuss to begin with? "They're getting even with you, Mother, for going on TV. Everyone wishes you'd cool it and let the proper authorities take charge. Jesus, Mother, next thing you know they'll come after Gideon and me and the kids!"

"But the authorities aren't doing anything, Adina. That's the point. Can't you see that if I don't speak up, those men will go on robbing your friends and you and the kids will always be in danger?" Mona is on the verge of tears. "No one will be safe until the men are caught—"

Adina has turned and is following Gideon out the front door.

31

A moment later

DON'T LEAVE! Mona wants to cry out.

Don't be silly, Mona, she scolds herself. They aren't leaving. They're going home to their children, which is where they belong.

With bucket and sponge, she hurries into the bathroom to wash away the toothpaste and for a moment the glass is smeared and the world is white and she is invisible.

She hears a man's voice singing softly behind the whiteness, opens the medicine cabinet. "Uncle Gabe, I know you're there." But all she can see is pieces of her own face reflected in the metal lining behind bottles of makeup and pills.

The bathroom reeks of sweet peppermint. She empties the cloudy water into the kitchen sink, shakes glass shards from the pictures of Izzy and Uncle Gabe, returns the pictures to the wall.

"John Shoemaker followed me up and down the mountain, and into my home," she tells Uncle Gabe's picture. "Gideon's right, you know. Shoemaker means to threaten my family."

Uncle Gabe steps out from under the photographer's cardboard tree to sit on the daybed where he sings a ballad about a gray-haired woman who wanders through a prickly abyss, caged in by mountains rising around her, by brambles tangled into eerie patterns overhead. Now comes a spindly man with a wide smile and yellowish horns and a beak-like nose. In terror, the woman flies wildly about, trying to escape this man whose beard bursts into flame, whose thin tail swishes furiously back and forth between his legs.

The man leaps out of the song and into view. "I know you, John Shoemaker," Mona cries. She runs to the kitchen, grabs a broom, and sweeps the shattered glass from the rug into a small pile.

"There is a mountain in the distance. Follow me to the top," the spindly man whispers in her ear. "If you stick to the path you are on, your skin will be ripped open by thorns, you will be overcome by noxious fumes, and a raven will eat you. Follow me. Grab the jasmine vine. Climb the mountain."

"Don't go! The perfumed path is treacherous," Uncle Gabe shouts, trembling with anger. "The sweet smells are poison gases. You are safer in the abyss."

"Stop! Both of you stop!" Mona cries. With the broom she sweeps the air. "Get out of my house, Mr. Shoemaker," she screams. "Get out!" And then she snaps at Uncle Gabe, "Look at this mess, will you. It's your fault."

She turns on the TV, which drinks up the light in the room. Relieved to be in semi-darkness, she collapses into the easy chair. All at once it occurs to her that she should not have washed the mirror. "How stupid, Mona," she groans. "You washed away hard evidence. Here you are dreaming dreams when you should be calling the police so they can get fingerprints and solve this mystery once and for all."

32

"I'VE NEVER BEEN so scared," Mona tells Dorothy and Sam. The depth of her fear is hard for her to describe. "It's like I'm being chased by Dracula and Frankenstein at the same time." It is worse than it was when Adina was so sick with pneumonia, worse than it was when she had so many miscarriages before Adina was born, worse than it was when she knew Izzy was dying. She felt alone then, but not stranded as she does now. Public officials will not listen to her. They tell the world she is crazy. At the market the other day Caroline Algren and Portia Twohy deliberately avoided her. Moses is moving away. Maryalice is threatening to exile her to the office. And her own children.... She cannot bear to think about her children. Even the valley is changing. The shopkeepers are putting in new security systems, the Torinos next door are talking about installing barbed wire on top of their fence, and just today Mona overheard a customer at Sam's saying the Victor's Grove residents were planning to build a security gate at the entrance to Bonanza Way. Dorothy and Sam, her dearest friends, cannot really understand what she is experiencing. Even in the warmth of this kitchen she feels alone. "Gideon is convinced I'm a meddling old woman," she whispers.

"You *are* a meddling old woman," Sam says softly. "There's nothing wrong with that, except that people don't like women to meddle, especially when they're old. They're afraid of old people because they're afraid of death."

Dorothy stares across the table at Sam. He is such a quiet man, a little like Leon, she thinks, so quiet you do not expect him to say anything terribly wise and you are surprised when all of a sudden he does.

"You know, honey," she says to Mona. "As I think about what you've been going through these past few weeks, it seems to me that you're being pursued by spirits from the past, by visions from lord knows which century. From what you tell me, it sounds like spirits from the past are battling for your soul."

"Spirits from the past visit me all the time," Sam says. "My Uncle Ibrahim says you have to meet the past before you can deal with the future." Sam grew up in Brooklyn and Uncle Ibrahim never misses an opportunity to tell him what he has missed, to urge him to return to Ramallah, to see his family home, the olive trees, the stone house, to visit the graveyard, to meet his relatives. At Uncle Ibrahim's insistence, Sam once began setting aside money for the trip, but then there were other more immediate needs.

Dorothy turns off the lights. A lopsided moon shines through the window.

"Uncle Gabe seems to think I'm safest if I keep going on, you know, if I don't hide, if I stay visible," Mona whispers.

"Maybe he wants you to call a press conference," Sam says.

"That's an idea," Dorothy agrees, "although we'll have to figure out how to get reporters to come. Even with this vandalism, they're going to remember what Salwen and Hambly said about Mona and they may not take her seriously." She takes Mona's hand. "I vote in favor of waiting for a more opportune time, but in the meantime we can tell everyone we know. Gossip works wonders. Reporters may not be interested in what you have to say, but there are other ways to broadcast news."

"You'll be safer that way," Sam says. "Shoemaker's smart enough to realize that he'd be taking a tremendous chance if he did anything more to harm you or your family."

Dorothy nods emphatically. "Meanwhile, Mona, you've told the police—"

"Yes, dear, they came and took photos, my statement."

"Didn't they take fingerprints?"

"They tried, said they couldn't find any. To tell you the truth, I don't think they were very interested. I certainly didn't have the feeling that they were going to do anything more than file a report."

"Well, that's not terribly surprising, is it?" Dorothy says. "Even if they don't do anything, it's important to have it on the record—"

"To have them know that *you* take it seriously," Sam agrees.

"Mona, why don't you stay over tonight? You can sleep on the sofa, you could stay with us for a few weeks, for that matter, you know, until this simmers down."

"Oh, thank you, Dorothy, but I have to be near Adina and the boys. I can't let it hang this way with her and Gideon mad at me."

"There's an irony having Gideon and Adina mad at you," Sam says. "I mean, on the one hand they accuse you of having an overactive imagination. They say Shoemaker's a fantasy, but then they're mad because they think that in trying to publicize what you overheard you invited the robbers to retaliate. Don't they realize they can't have it both ways? Why would the robbers threaten you unless they knew you were dangerously close to the truth?"

Mona nods. Obviously that is why they ransacked her cottage. Mona cannot understand why Gideon does not see this. "Why isn't he mad at Shoemaker, or at the police for letting this happen?"

"He's not thinking, honey. He's acting out of fear. His reflexes are running his brain. They're telling him if he closes his eyes Shoemaker will go away. They're saying you're the threat. They're telling him if he keeps up appearances he'll be able to build his damn jail."

"Dorothy's right, Mona. Gideon's trying to ingratiate himself with county officials. He's probably out of a job if he alienates the sheriff." Sam shrugs. "You have to consider too, Mona, that it's possible he doesn't want the robberies to stop. To some extent they work in his favor."

"Maybe he's working along with Shoemaker is what Sam means," Dorothy says.

"Oh, I don't think so, Sam. Gideon's got his faults. I mean, I'm glad I'm not married to him, but he's not working with Shoemaker. He doesn't even know Shoemaker. That's ridiculous."

"No, I doubt that he's part of the plot," Dorothy mutters. "I doubt that he has the imagination for that."

"If he's not one of them, he's in the bleachers cheering," Leon says. Leon, in denim pants and a denim jacket, is home from work, leaning against the kitchen door. "I mean, man, how can the supervisors turn down the money for a new jail, with a crime wave at Christmastime?"

"Oh, Leon!" Mona blurts out, surprised by the force of her words. "All of you! The supervisors don't need a crime wave. They're going to rent out cells to other counties. Gideon's a hard-working husband and a good provider and he comes from a nice family. He can't help it if sometimes he gets nervous."

33

SAM SAYS, "I had a funny dream last night. I was sitting in an arena, a huge coliseum, tier after tier. It was as big as the stadium in Harrison and so old the stone had turned into glass. Below on the dusty floor were my father, my grandfather, my great-grandfather, and a bunch of soldiers, a Roman soldier, a British soldier, an Israeli soldier. They were charging at one another, their bronze swords crashing against bronze shields, cutting the dusty air. High above, way out in the bleachers, my Grandfather Ismail sat playing a harp and singing. I was scared, so I hid in the bullpen. A man flew down one of the aisles. His beard flew behind him."

"Did the man have a long hooked nose?" Mona asks.

Sam nods. "His nose was an eagle's beak, an Arab's nose."

"Was his beard on fire?"

"Yes—Mona, how did you know?"

"I'm wondering that, myself," Dorothy says.

"Did Grandfather Ismail shout at you to cross the stadium?"

Again Sam nods. Dorothy is speechless. Mona lights a candle, waves it in the air.

"Mona, quit your jivin," Leon grumbles.

"No, let her finish."

"You started running up the steps," Mona goes on. "You were going to take the circular path along the top tier, until Grandfather Ismail called out to you, 'Sam, don't climb to the top. The high road is dangerous—'"

"Grandfather Ismail said, 'The stones at the top are fragile. They will crumble. You will fall and be killed—'"

"He told you to climb down instead. Climb to the bottom, walk through the battle—"

"Grandfather Ismail said, 'Experience the battle—'"

"He said it was the only safe way—"

"He said it was the only safe way—"

"Oh, Sam, I know because I've had the same vision." She recites Uncle Gabe's song.

"Ain't that some shit," Leon murmurs. He kicks a chair over to the table and sits down.

"You two are connected," Dorothy says. "Deeply connected. You must realize that. Let me get the wine bottle. This is an important event."

It is a deep connection, Sam realizes, because dreams and visions are lodged deep inside, deep in the past. They are the substance of human experience.

 34

All Saints Convalescent Home,
Monday, December 15

THE PATIENTS ARE having their Christmas party and Maryalice, in white rayon, glides around the circle of wheelchairs in the all-purpose room, waving a silver wand, extracting wishes.

Mona enters, clad in a scarlet cloak and turquoise boots, silver bells at the tips of her fingers. She twirls past wheelchairs, into the center of the circle. On her bosom is a gold pin, a yellow ring. "Merry Christmas, Helen, Shirley." She waves at the patients, but the patients play with noisemakers and do not seem to notice. Louise Simmons, a young matron, a new volunteer, takes Shirley's hand. Maryalice distributes silver-wrapped candy.

Mona spent the afternoon helping Debbie complete the December insurance forms, and Friday she was bent over a typewriter for hours, like an old lady tatting lace. Maryalice gave her these assignments, orders really, knowing Mona cannot type—and even if she could, Maryalice knows this is the sort of work she hates. Moses is leaving and Maryalice is taking charge.

"Merry Christmas, Shirley." Mona waves again. Now Shirley looks up but seems confused. Mona has been confined to the office for a week. Has Shirley forgotten who she is? Mona dances a little, gives Shirley a hug, stops to say hello to Lil.

"Take off that bloody Jew badge," Lil whispers.

"Jew badge?" Mona does not know what Lil means.

Lil jabs a finger at the gold pin. She spins around to drive her wheelchair to the back of the room.

Mona calls after her, "I don't know what you mean, Lil!" What's the fuss? It's a harmless pin. She runs her finger around the edge. Adina and Gideon gave it to her two Christmases ago, said they found it on sale at Magnin's. "It's twenty-four karat gold," Mona shouts. She stomps her feet and the room is suddenly silent. She slips out of the cloak and boots, unpins her hair, letting the silver braid fall onto her pale blue leotard.

Barefooted, she returns to the center of the circle. She twirls, and as the braid unravels, a story unravels, a story she has never heard but somehow knows, a story of Lilith who, with long hair and feathery wings, taunted young men as they slept alone, sprinkled her body with their spent seed, flew among the clouds as demons dropped from between her legs, clawed newborn children with sharp fingers then sucked the blood, hid under Salome's sarong and under the cloak of the Queen of Sheba, nourished the holy spirit of the blue Shekhina. The story is half spoken, half sung. Shirley stares with uncomprehending eyes. From the back of the room comes the sound of Lil's gruff laughter.

Maryalice is at the back of the room too, spooning punch into styrofoam cups. She recognizes Mona's purse on the floor, sets down the ladle, looks quickly around. Reassured that everyone is watching Mona, she opens the purse and riffles through the wallet, cannot find what she wants, closes the wallet, opens it again, pulls out a photo of Moses, tears the photo in half, tucks the pieces into her bosom.

Carrying a pink frosted angel food cake, she tiptoes to the center of the circle where she cuts off Mona's song with the opening bars of "Rudolph the Red-Nosed Reindeer." "Come on now, boys and girls, you've got to help me," she says and a crackly Rudolph chorus fills the room.

Mona is outraged by Maryalice's boldness, but she responds with a smile, since to challenge Maryalice now would only upset the patients, and so she steps outside the circle of wheelchairs and joins Lil in the back of the room.

"Maryalice has me on the outside too, Lil," Mona says.

"That's where Jews belong."

Mona smiles. "Maybe you're right." She watches Maryalice still singing and trotting around with the cake. "I think it's time for me to leave, to volunteer at another nursing home, the Good Shepherd in Rancho, or Fowler's in Lexington. The tension between Maryalice and me isn't good for the patients. But I want you to know, Lil, that if I do decide to leave I'll still have plenty of time to come and visit you."

"Maryalice dropped her eyeball into your purse," Lil mumbles.

Lil hasn't heard a word I said, Mona tells herself. "That's all right, dear. I don't mind," she says aloud, and she takes Lil's hand.

 35

MONA IS ANGRY at Moses for keeping his plans a secret, as Moses knew she would be, although he did not expect her anger to last so long. In a purple top and rhinestone-studded jeans, she is bent over the kitchen counter, wrapping coffee mugs in newspaper. He lifts her hair—she is wearing it loose—and kisses the back of her neck. She pulls away.

"Damn it, Moses, I'm angry. Can't you even take my anger seriously?"

What does she want, he wonders. He told her he was sorry. He can't undo what is done. He told her he loved her. "What do you want me to say?"

"Oh, how do I know what I want you to say? I want to know that you see me."

"I do see you, although I must confess I'm not sure at this moment who you are. You're certainly not the woman I met three years ago. You actually look younger somehow."

He is obviously sad and instinctively she wants to console him. What else can she do? She hugs him until he relaxes into her bosom. The overture to *Die Valkyrie* plays in the background.

"Moses, you're not going to believe this, but Lil told me I should sit on top of you when we're having sex. She was quite adamant about it."

"Lil said that to you?" Moses grins. "Did you tell her we do it that way all the time?"

"I told her and she became very impatient with me, said I should sit up straight and look down on you like an Egyptian queen. She said that way the tingles last longer—those were her exact words."

He laughs. "I wonder if she's right. We'll have to try it. You've worked miracles with Lil, you know," he tells her. "No one else has been able to get her to utter a word. Dr. Engleberger and Maryalice have it written in stone that she's hopelessly catatonic when it's obvious that she's very much alive. For some reason I'm reminded of the story of Lilith. Do you know that story?"

There he goes again with another one of his stories. Mona sighs. He is pretending everything is as it was before, when they both know tonight is a parting. He insists nothing will change, they will see each other on weekends, but he will be moving tomorrow and tonight is the end of their affair. He wants to hang loose, he has always said so, and it is odd because she is coming to realize that maybe she does too. With all his faults, he is a kind and good person and she loves him still. The trouble is though that she has to conceal so much of herself when they are together. Maybe she would be happier alone for a while, or with another man. "It's odd that you should mention Lilith because I recently had a vision about a woman by the same name."

"Lilith was Adam's first wife. According to legend, God fashioned her from earth, along with Adam. She was dark and slender and she pleased Adam, at least until the day they were making love and she insisted on being on top. 'God has decreed that I'm supposed to be on top,' Adam told her, but Lilith refused to budge, and Adam could think of no way to regain control except to appeal to heaven. Naturally God was upset when he learned that Lilith had disobeyed his law, and he sternly advised her to reform. Lilith was hunched over, picking gooseberries at the time and instead of standing in God's presence, she merely looked up at him and burst out laughing. Of course that only enraged him more, and so he cursed her, told her all her children would either die at birth or turn into demons. He snapped his fingers and she flew off into the sky."

"I would have laughed too. I mean, who is God to interfere in a personal relationship? Although it was pretty nice of him to give her the wherewithal to fly. I'd love to fly, over the chimneytops, you know. I'd love to play violin duets with Uncle Gabe—"

"Uncle Gabe?"

"My mother's uncle. I've told you about him, the one who brought me presents when I was a girl? Once, you know, he brought me a rocking horse. My mother grumbled, 'What does a child need with such an expensive toy?' She was terribly angry, I think, and I wonder now if she was afraid that the rocking horse would carry me away from her harsh scrutiny. I wonder if she was afraid the horse might teach me to fly."

She has not told Moses what happened on Sunday, but she does now. "I didn't think people drew swastikas any more," she tells him. She has had time to absorb the shock of having her home violated, or at least to bury it, so that she speaks calmly and she is surprised by Moses's reaction.

"You're in terrible danger!" he tells her. She has never seen his face so pained. He is shouting, on the verge of tears. He tells her she cannot go home, not until Shoemaker is safely in jail, she should stay with Dorothy, live with her for a while, or come with him to North City. He tells her the toothpaste pig was the Judensau, a cartoon character from hundreds of years ago. "The pig is meant to be Jewish. It's a dirty, disgusting animal. Ancient cartoons had Jews suckling the pig and eating her excrement. Jews were ugly men with big crooked noses. They wore Jew badges, and some had horns and long tails like the Devil."

"What's a Jew badge?" This is what Lil called the gold pin Mona wore to the Christmas party.

"Badges Jews were forced to wear during the Middle Ages, to identify who they were. Some were yellow circles like your pin. Hitler revived the custom when he made Jews wear the Star of David."

"Those are terrible stories, Moses."

"They're not stories!" Moses's voice is trembling. This horror could have happened yesterday, the emotion behind his words is so intense. "I don't think you know what it means to be Jewish!" he says angrily.

"But, Moses, that's ridiculous. I've been Jewish all my life."

He shakes his head. "Whatever you were taught when you were a child you've long forgotten. You've lived in Jasmine for too long."

Mona wishes Moses had not told her about the Judensau. He has shattered the fragile sense of security she worked all day to achieve, and she tries vainly to erase the image from her mind, calling up gentle memories of Uncle Gabe playing his violin, Izzy tossing Adina in the air. The Judensau remains before her. She tries to stare it away, but the more she stares the clearer it becomes, until she has the decided impression that she has seen this animal before. She has seen its repulsive snout and its snake-like tail. "I've always known you," she whispers to the Judensau, and now she remembers the day Shoemaker first came into Sam's, his long shadowy body. She remembers the sense she had that they too had met before.

36

ERVINA BOUDREAU, an attractive woman who wears tailored skirts and pale silk blouses, has been librarian ever since Andrew and Ian have been borrowing books. "How are Adina and the boys?" she asks, as she always does when she sees Mona, although this evening she does not wait for the answer because she is eager to know if Mona has heard about the holdups.

Mona hands Ervina the book she is returning for Andrew on her way home from work and replies, "I'm not sure what you mean by holdups."

"Armed robberies," Ervina explains. She tells Mona that Jess Haley was held up at gunpoint on his own front lawn in Victor's Grove. He was trimming the hedges when a man wearing an ankle-length cloak and a hangman's hood brandished a gun and demanded money. This happened so quickly that Jess's wife, who was inside taking a shower at the time, never heard a thing, and an hour later a cloaked and hooded man held up Pricilla Brady at knifepoint.

"So it's come to that," Mona murmurs.

"To what, Mona?"

"Burglars, swastikas, guns, and knives."

"Swastikas?"

Mona looks at Ervina for a long moment. She is a nice woman. Mona has always liked her, and it occurs to her that she is the perfect person to spread the word about what happened on Sunday, since in the course of a week she is in contact with half the families in Jasmine.

Frowning occasionally, occasionally seeming actually annoyed, Ervina listens as Mona tells her story. Is Ervina angry at what Shoemaker did, Mona wonders, or does she think Mona is crazy?

Ervina does not say. "I saw J.C. Heilbron a few minutes ago," she announces abruptly once Mona has finished, as if one good story deserves another. "Ran into him this morning on my way to work. He says he's positive some gang from Lexington is committing the robberies. I don't know where he got his information. I'd thought the robbers had kept themselves pretty invisible, but J.C. said that's who they were and that everything was Mayor Hambly's fault. He said Hambly should have put more cops on patrol, especially at the northern border, said he was going to have Hambly recalled if he has to do it single-handed. I imagine he'll run for mayor himself and use the campaign to force the county to expand the sheriff's department and build the new jail."

"J.C." Mona repeats the name, which is poised uncomfortably somewhere at the edge of her memory.

"You know J.C. Heilbron, Mona. He's lived in Jasmine longer than I have."

"I think I know who he is."

"He's a real estate broker in Jasmine Village, a developer. He was involved in the Rancho-Jasmine development a few years back. He kept himself pretty invisible, but everyone knew he was a prime backer."

"Yes, I think I've seen his name in the paper," although this is not what Mona is trying to remember. She has heard the name J.C. recently in some other context. She closes her eyes, trying to prod her memory. The image of an olive branch comes to mind, and she associates this with Sam's. What does Sam's have to do with J.C.? She shrugs. The memory will come to her later.

She got off work early tonight, and the sky outside is pinkish around the setting sun. As she descends the stairs to the street, she notices a hand-painted "Recall Hambly" sign on the lawn in front of the law offices next to the post office. It was not there minutes ago when she went into the library.

She hurries down Apricot Avenue, all lined with turn-of-the-century pastel Victorians that now house Jasmine's tiny assortment of governmental offices. The street is almost deserted and the pads of Mona's walking shoes crunch on gravel as she turns down Orchard Lane towards Whitticomb's Market.

She is so busy trying to remember where she recently heard J.C.'s name that she does not notice Ray Niegarth, Portia Twohy, and Caroline Algren until they are about to pass her.

Ray is saying, "Isn't it just like Hambly to be on vacation at a time like this?"

Caroline says, "He's incompetent. I don't think anyone's run against him since he first was elected mayor."

Portia says, "I can't understand why he hasn't acted. It's been clear for two weeks that we need reinforcements for the border patrol."

Caroline says, "I'm certainly glad to see J.C. taking the lead. We need someone with muscle to take over."

Passing in front of Mona, they turn their heads away.

"I spoke up weeks ago," she calls after them. "Why didn't you listen then?"

They pretend not to hear, continue on towards the market.

"That was a ridiculous story Mona told about real estate developers planning to rob our houses," Caroline says loudly.

Portia replies, "It was crazy. The robbers are obviously Blacks from Lexington."

Ray proclaims, with a sardonic laugh, "Of course they are. Businessmen don't use knives."

"They don't use knives unless they want you to think they're Blacks from Lexington," Mona shouts after them.

37

Point Crespi Aquarium,
Thursday afternoon, December 18

MONA AND ADINA hang over an iron railing, gazing down into a misty tidal pool where starfish move in slow motion. "Wouldn't one of them make a spectacular medallion to wear with my Liz Claiborne sweater?" Adina murmurs. "Or two, for a pair of earrings?" She touches her earlobes, imagining the faint pink against her turquoise eyes.

Mona smiles in response. Even in beat-up sweat pants, Adina looks gorgeous. The starfish color would be stunning against her olive skin. A pair of cormorants catches Mona's eye. They look a little like sleepy vultures, squatting on rocks at the mouth of the bay, twisting their long necks in rhythm to the sea, and slowly she backs away from Adina, following the iron fence to a point where the birds are in sharper focus and she can clearly see them preening their windblown feathers. She loses herself in their world until the air feels suddenly chilly. She hurries inside.

In summer the aquarium lures tourists from all over the world, but now, so close to Christmas, Mississippi sweat shirts and flowered shorts and chartreuse sandals are absent, and so is the incessant chatter. Gideon and the boys are in a small balcony watching the silver-headed sea otters being fed. The boys' excited cries carry over the soft jingle of Christmas music. Even the squish of Mona's tennis shoes is clearly audible on the granite floor. She passes a cluster of display tanks arranged in an L, stops to watch a family of bat rays flying evenly spaced in endless circles through dark water.

The delicate tread of Adina's athletic shoes follows. Adina gasps in horror at an octopus embalmed and packed into a tall jar. She hurries into a stucco tunnel where she is surrounded by rosy fish swimming in green water. Taking this trip to Point Crespi was Gideon's idea, a chance to get away from the pressures of work for a couple of days, he told Adina, to get away from worrying about vandals too. It would be a good break, he said, for the two of them, and for Mona and the boys. It would be a chance to talk things over, to come to some agreement. Gideon sat on the edge of their bed talking softly as Adina, surrounded by pillows, unhappily sorted through a box of pictures of herself as a child.

Adina pushes a button on the display case, which causes the water in the tank to bubble and churn like a witch's cauldron. She enjoys the game, repeats it after the water calms.

She steps forward to peer at her face reflected in the glass. Gideon says she is beginning to resemble her mother. Can't he see that her nose is straighter, and her skin is lighter? Perhaps he would like her better if she dyed her hair blond.

Mona stands before the embalmed octopus whose tendrils stretch upwards as if it is praying to God for release. "I know how you feel, kiddo," she says. She wanders off to the far side of the building, to the side opposite where Adina is standing. She thinks about the drive down, all of them playing the license plate game, Ian winning, as he always does, finding cars from sixteen different states. After the boys tired of games, the conversation became strained and Mona dozed off to escape from the tension. Things will be better tonight, she tells herself. Gideon and the boys will play Clue in the cabin, and she and Adina will have time to talk.

She approaches a tank filled with tiny fish weaving in and out of jack-in-the-beanstalk seaweed beneath sunlit bubbles, is enchanted by the orange anemones and maroon starfish and lavender barnacles in the tank next door, a velvet underwater world, Edith's Thrift Shop on Blossom Street sunk to the bottom of the sea. The shellfish wear lapis lazuli earrings, and hermit crabs wear pea green turbans, and seaweed wafts back and forth in an unseen breeze.

She pushes the button, watches bubbles explode through the tank and color disappear. Behind the bubbles she is certain she sees a pair of human eyes. Someone is watching the same display from the other side. The bubbles settle, the eyes are gone, and she hurries around the end of the row of tanks to see who it is, but no one is there when she turns the corner. It was only Gideon, she reassures herself as her anxiety grows.

The boys stand gaping at the bat rays. Mona passes them by, runs to the center of the cavernous building where she finds Gideon and Adina side by side holding hands. "Aren't the fish beautiful?" she asks weakly.

Gideon nods.

"Adina tells me you've got the votes," Mona blurts out.

"The votes?" Gideon looks startled.

"Yes, the board of supervisors. She says you'll be chosen to design the new county jail!"

Adina stares at Mona in horror, and Mona bites her tongue, realizing that she promised Adina not to tell anyone she knew this secret, least of all Gideon. She had to say something, though, to cut the tension.

Gideon does not seem to mind that Mona knows. In fact he seems to welcome the opening to say, "I expect to get the job unless something goes wrong."

"What could possibly go wrong?" Mona asks.

"The supervisors may decide we don't have the money for a jail after all. The county engineers may decide they like someone else's work better than mine after all, or maybe they'll decide they don't like me."

"That's silly. Why wouldn't they like you?"

"It's not silly, Mother!" Adina cries. "Are you blind and deaf? Do you really have to ask? Don't you know that Gideon's afraid he may be in trouble because of the fuss you've been making about these robberies? He's afraid they'll say that if he can't keep his crazy mother-in-law in tow, maybe he should do business in a different county. Caroline thinks you're a meddling old woman, sticking your big nose where it doesn't belong—"

"But Adina, Gideon isn't me. If people don't like me—"

"It reflects on him, Mom. Why can't you see that? Don't you ever care what people think?" Adina is shouting. "Don't you know that your appearance is gross, Mother? You wear those sleazy outfits to work. Every year they get worse and worse. People used to think you were quaint. Now they think you're crazy. Caroline says you look like a Jewish Mary Poppins when you ride your bicycle, and who but Mona Pinsky would befriend the only Black working in Orchard Valley?"

"Adina!"

"Gideon thinks you should publicly apologize to Sheriff Salwen for embarrassing him, and maybe you should go live with Dorothy in Lexington!" Adina is screaming.

"Live with Dorothy? I live in *my* house." Adina and Gideon live in her house too. She owns the title, all the land. Someday it will belong to them, but how can Gideon even consider inviting her to move away from the house she and Izzy worked so hard to buy?

"Do you think I should move, Adina?"

"Do I think?" Adina stops short because she is unused to being asked her opinion. "I think it would be a good idea if you moved out," she finally says, softly, "at least until Gideon's employment is resolved. And I think you should see someone too, Mom, you know—"

SOME THINGS ARE so upsetting they are best pushed away, then allowed to return slowly so that they can be absorbed a little at a time. Mona and Dorothy are spending Sunday and Monday at Reno—they planned the trip a few weeks ago—and Mona is determined not to let herself think about what happened at the Point Crespi Aquarium, not until they have returned. For safety's sake, to keep Shoemaker off their trail, they have not told anyone where they are going, except of course Leon and Sam. Adina and Gideon think Mona will be spending the time in North City.

Mona is at the daybed, unpacking the canvas bag she had at Point Crespi, so eager to leave for Reno she is packing a larger overnight bag at the same time. Some of the items she merely transfers from bag to bag (the toothbrush and toothpaste), but she must return the Point Crespi wardrobe to the closet and replace it with bold casino attire. As she crosses the room she holds a pair of sweats off to one side and turns her head to the other, afraid she will discover the sound of Adina's fury lodged in the folds. Throughout this ritual, she is aware of Uncle Gabe hovering beneath the ceiling beams like a wingless bird.

"How can you be so calm, Uncle Gabe, when the world is falling apart?" Mona shouts. "Shoemaker shadows me up mountains, inside revolving doors. He steals Christmas presents from my daughter's good friend, and in case that isn't enough, he holds people up at gunpoint, robs them at home when their wives are taking showers. Now he comes and vandalizes my house, terrorizes my family. I tell the police. They don't care. They investigate and nothing happens. I tell the politicians. They shake my hand, denounce me in public. Reporters don't want the story. They refuse to answer my calls. My daughter's best friend is snubbing me, and my daughter and son-in-law...." She tears the nightgown from the canvas bag, rolls it into a ball, and stuffs it into the Reno bag. Uncle Gabe floats down onto the daybed. "Why don't you..." she begins, but the thought dissolves when Uncle Gabe disappears behind an octopus who has lavender freckles and eight watery blue eyes.

Uncle Gabe reappears near the window. He pulls a violin from his hip pocket, sets it firmly between his chin and shoulder and, leaning back against the sill, he sings the ballad of the prickly abyss.

"You and your damned prickly abyss," Mona grumbles. She tosses a packet of Kleenex towards the dining room table. It misses the mark and lands on the floor near Adina's chair. She hurries across the room, pushes the chair out of view, near the kitchen sink, returns to her packing.

Uncle Gabe's singing grows louder and more insistent. He has changed some of the words of his song, has planted an olive tree among the thistles on the valley floor.

"Damned olive tree," Mona mumbles. She shuts her eyes, but the tree remains. Uncle Gabe has taken the tree from Sam's, she realizes. It belongs in the entryway where it has always been, where it was the first day Shoemaker and his friends came into the restaurant, immaculately dressed in gabardine suits, seeming to enjoy the crowded ambiance, the noise, probably because they thought no one would be able to hear them when they plotted their upsetting crimes.... "That's where I heard J.C.'s name," Mona whispers.

Uncle Gabe stops singing.

"'J.C. wants it done before Christmas when it will be most upsetting.' That's what they said." It was always obvious that J.C. was preying on people's fears to get himself elected, but it never occurred to Mona until just now that he would pay Shoemaker and his friends to create fear by breaking into people's homes, by holding them up, by vandalizing trees, by drawing swastikas and pigs. "J.C. hired Shoemaker to create a crime wave, Uncle Gabe. He planted fear and cultivated it by plastering posters all over town and circulating recall petitions. He did all this to lure people onto his law-and-order bandwagon and make them forget his developer ties."

Uncle Gabe smiles his crooked smile and shrugs. "Nu, stranger things have happened," he says, and like a clown on a trampoline, he jumps off the bed and floats out the window, drifting towards the waning moon. His face is green and his crooked nose tilts to one side.

"What should I do?" Mona shouts after him. "Even if I'm right, who will believe me?" She starts for the phone to call Dorothy but hears a crackling sound beneath the window and drops the receiver to hurry to the daybed and peer outside. Although it is foggy and the glass is steamy, she is certain she sees a familiar pair of bluish eyes. Shoemaker? No, it has to be Gideon. Gideon must be watching. Has he been standing outside all this time? God forbid, has he overheard her conversation with Uncle Gabe?

She runs out the door intending to confront him. If he was there a minute ago, he is gone now. I know you're trying to frighten me off, Gideon! she wants to shout, but if she did the Torinos would hear and Adina would be mad.

She hears the crackling sound again and now something soft brushes against her leg—grass, dandelion fluff. She looks down. "Zebadiah?" She bends over to stroke the cat, to enjoy the reassurance of his hard body beneath the fur. He purrs. He swishes his crooked tail and pulls away and darts off into the chaparral.

 39

All Saints Convalescent Home,
Saturday morning, December 20

"WE'VE SOLVED THE mystery, Lil." Mona describes the cynical plot. "Dorothy thinks J.C. is somehow involved in the Adobe Reservoir development project too. She says he's in it up to his gills, there has to be the connection, with Jasmine and Lexington being so close, so we're asking Sam to find money to hire Joe Bourne to investigate. And something sort of weird, Lil. Dorothy thinks the anti-Semitism was fake—not the swastikas, they were real, and the pig, but she says J.C. had Shoemaker draw them not because he hates Jews, but to call attention to my Jewishness, to stir up anti-Semitic feeling in the community, you know, the same way politicians use Blacks."

"Evil..." Lil says. The word rattles her chest.

Mona nods. "It is evil, truly evil. I mean, not even their badness is sincere. It's funny though because on the one hand I'm horrified, but I'm exhilarated too. I mean I've solved a mystery, Lil. Sure, I've solved TV mysteries before, but never a real one, so it's all very exciting and frightening—and it's sad too because Adina thinks I'm an embarrassment to her and Gideon and she wants me to move away, she wants me to move away from the house that's been home for forty years. She wants to get rid of me, like Arline got rid of you. I try not to think about it. Dorothy's offered to put me up for a while—"

"Say no," Lil sputters.

Mona cleans the drool off Lil's face.

"Say no," Lil persists.

"I'll try to."

"...promise."

"Lil, I can't promise because I don't know if I have the courage to insist on living where I'm not wanted. I don't know if I'm strong enough to risk completely alienating my daughter."

"...bad example," Lil gasps.

I can't always set a good example, I'm not that strong, Mona wants to say, but she realizes that Lil looks terribly weak tonight and her skin is yellow. This is no time for such a serious discussion. "There's going to be a new moon tonight," she tells Lil. "There was a new moon the first day I saw Shoemaker in Sam's. I know I'm right because it was the same day Zebadiah disappeared. Funny, it's been only four weeks, a moon month. It feels like an eon."

"You've been on a journey," Lil whispers.

"You're right, I have been on a journey and I don't think it's over."

Lil laughs.

"What's funny, Lil?"

Lil's laugh dissolves into violent coughing and Mona jumps up, alarmed at how Lil has to struggle simply to lift her head. When Lil's coughing subsides, Mona whispers, "I'm going to get the nurse, dear."

Lil grabs her hand. "Don't go—"

"Oh, sweetheart, I'm not going to leave you, but I'm afraid. You seem so frail." Mona is crying. Lil is old tonight, much older than she has ever been before. Her voice is a silver wisp, and she is lying so still with the sheet and two blankets pulled up to her chin that her head seems dismembered from her skinny body.

The two women stare at one another as if their eyes are joined. "I *have* been on a journey, Lil. I've climbed mountains and descended into valleys. Being at Point Crespi with Adina and Gideon was like climbing a burning tree."

"Were there apples on the tree?" Lil asks so softly Mona must bend over to hear. Her tears spill onto Lil's face, settling into the delicate cracks. "The tree was dripping with apples. How did you know?"

"Tree of knowledge..." Lil gasps.

"Won't you let me get the nurse, dear?"

Lil tightens her grasp. "You've been on your journey. Let me go on mine," she says with amazing clarity. She closes her eyes but soon her mouth smiles and again she is laughing.

"What do you see, Lil?"

"Uncle Gabe."

"Is he playing his violin?"

"No...standing under the tree of life."

"The tree of life? Is that the same as the tree of knowledge?"

Lil coughs. "...no apples...grows upside down."

"Upside down? With its roots in the sky?"

"Heaven."

"Its roots are in heaven, no less. That's some tree, Lil. What's Uncle Gabe doing?"

"Waiting...for me."

"He's waiting for you?"

"Horny."

"Uncle Gabe's horny? What an evil thing to say. You're pulling my leg, Lilith...don't look startled, I know who you are. Moses told me all about you."

Lil is obviously pleased. She laughs, coughs. Her face goes blue.

Sobbing, Mona pushes down on her chest. "I have to get the nurse, Lil."

The coughing stops. Again Lil grabs Mona's hand. "Picnic basket."

"Oh, I see, you and Uncle Gabe are going to have a picnic under the tree of life. What's in the basket?"

"Barbecued Judensau."

"Barbecued Judensau?" Mona bursts out laughing. "That's one way to get rid of the monster. Maybe I'll barbecue Shoemaker next time I see him."

Lil laughs too. The smile in front of her laugh consumes her face.

The laughing stops. The smile freezes. Mona sits by the bed for a long while, unable to relinquish the cold hand.

ALTHOUGH THE EMERGENCY meeting of the Jasmine Town Council was not announced until four o'clock over cable news,
council chambers have never been so crowded. The Channel
Fifty-Three camera crew is on hand, the seating area is full,
and people are jammed three deep at the back of the room.
Jasmine's public officials usually represent their constituents
quietly, behind closed doors, and the room's richly oiled redwood paneling, its floor-to-ceiling windows and crystal chandelier seem more suited for business meetings than political
debate. Mayor Hambly, stiff on a high-back chair, half hidden
behind a mahogany desk, looks more like a corporate executive than a politician. So do the two council members on either side of him.

Mona and Dorothy and Sam arrived early to get seats near
the front—Sam here tonight in the role of a longtime valley
merchant, Dorothy a political leader from a neighboring community. Mona has submitted the required speaker's card and
is going to address the council. She was going to wear the
gold lamé pantsuit she packed for Reno but then she heard
the sound of Adina's anger and switched to her Sunday suit.
It is a shock being here surrounded by so much noise and
excitement after resting at home for most of the afternoon,
trying to understand that Lil was dead, realizing it would be
weeks before the idea took hold, before she would get out of
the habit of driving by the convalescent home to look in on
her friend. She cried a lot, but felt happy too, knowing Lil had
taken her freedom.

Mayor Hambly is just off the plane, back from a vacation
in Bali, and despite the strain he must feel, he looks tanned

and relaxed. He calls the meeting to order, but his businessman's voice is inaudible over the din. Even the council members do not seem to hear him as they pore over manila folders stuffed with papers.

Hambly pulls a wooden gavel from his desk drawer, bangs it repeatedly on the green blotter pad, until the room grows quiet and everyone stands to pledge allegiance to the flag. "This meeting has been called out of concern over the burglaries we've been having. We are determined to devise a plan to stop them before they turn into something serious," he says. "Never in my ten years in office, or in my thirty-two years as a resident of Jasmine, has this town had to consider the problem of crime. Under these circumstances your concern is natural, and I want you all to rest assured that the county police and I are working together, doing all that can possibly be done."

He tells the audience he has contacted the FBI. By now everyone is losing patience. Murmurs swell into outspoken words until someone calls out, "We want J.C," and others join in.

Hambly begins to say, "Now isn't the time for speakers," but he stops short, obviously aware of how bad it would look for him not to let J.C. speak, especially since J.C. has risen from his front-row seat and is slowly walking towards the rostrum.

J.C. takes the microphone from the stand, turns his back on the mayor and council, and addresses the crowd, saying that just this afternoon driving down Orchard Avenue he noticed that so many jasmine vines on the hillsides were dying. "The time for change has arrived," he says. It is time to elect a man who will bring new leadership to the sheriff's department, what the town of Jasmine needs is a new sheriff and a new county jail.

The audience applauds. Vainly Hambly pounds the gavel. His calm facade has dissolved, revealing the reddened face of a man who is deeply shaken. "I feel sorry for him," Mona whispers. "He probably isn't the strongest person for the job, but he certainly doesn't deserve this."

When Dorothy called to tell Mona about the emergency meeting, Mona found herself immediately volunteering to get up and speak. Her decision came so easily it did not feel like a decision at all. Perhaps Lil telling her that she had to set an example made it so easy to decide, or perhaps it was Sam telling her that the best way to prevent Shoemaker from doing her further violence was to expose him to the public eye. Sam said that neither Shoemaker nor J.C. were likely to harm her after she publicly accused them, and she is convinced that tonight represents an important opportunity to be heard, although she is not completely sure where she will find the ability to speak. The only time in her life she spoke in public was when she stood to give a report on Navajo basket-making before Mrs. Katz's fifth-grade class and then she was so nervous she went mute. If she could not find the words to address her classmates, where will she find them now?

"Look at J.C., will you? He looks like John Wayne," Dorothy says. "Look at him swaggering, so big and tall, showing off his muscles, his black linen suit, his black string tie."

"I bet J.C.'s got a holster on his belt," Sam murmurs.

"And a whip tucked inside his pants," Dorothy adds. "Look at him. He's having a ball." J.C. has stepped down from the podium. He is standing off to the side, his neck twisted awkwardly so the audience can see the regular lines of his profile.

"Two years ago everyone was terrified of the developers, said they were trying to destroy the community," Sam says.

"Now it's crime they're afraid of and, man, they love J.C. because he looks like John Wayne. He could talk gibberish and people would follow him."

"You're right," Mona says. "I think they're forever afraid. They hide in their backyards. They hide when there's nothing to hide from, and then they're helpless when the danger's real and they look for someone strong." She looks at the faces around her, most of them young.

Reluctantly Mayor Hambly takes up a stack of speakers' cards. Now is not the point in the agenda when citizens ordinarily address the council, but in deference to the crowd he begins calling out the names of residents who have signed up to be heard.

Caroline Algren speaks first, saying she represents the newer residents of Jasmine who, having sacrificed so much to live where they do, now find themselves afraid to come home at night. The audience listens attentively and applauds.

Portia Twohy says she speaks for Jasmine's business community when she says that this is the slowest Christmas she can remember, and she is afraid if Mayor Hambly does not step down and let a younger more energetic man take over, the crime wave will continue and the town of Jasmine will die. Again the audience applauds.

Ray Niegarth says that everyone knows where these robbers come from. The border patrol needs to be expanded. The audience cheers.

When Mona hears her name called, she hurries down the aisle. She has rehearsed in her mind what she is going to say, but now as she approaches the rostrum she feels her stomach tighten. What are you doing here, you crazy old fool? she mutters to herself. You saw how the crowd treated the mayor. How do you think they'll treat you? She is about to turn around and head back to her seat, but something—a voice, a feeling—restrains her. She takes a deep breath, holds the microphone up to her lips, and says, "Good evening, ladies and gentlemen." She is addressing the mayor and council. Her voice is shaking and it seems as though the entire audience is talking behind her. Somewhere she finds the presence of mind to pivot until simply by turning her head she can talk in both directions, like actresses she has seen.

The audience is too large and she is too nervous to be able to make out individual faces, although she can clearly see the shadowy form of a spindly man standing in the back of the room behind the wooden railing. How brash of Shoemaker to show up tonight! He obviously is trying to scare her into silence. As if reading her mind, he leans forward, thrusting his smiling face into the oval of light cast by the chandelier.

"Mrs. Pinsky, are you going to speak?" Mayor Hambly asks impatiently.

"Yes, of course I'm going to speak," she says, relieved that her voice is stronger. She squeezes the microphone, as J.C. did, until the skin covering her hands is smooth and the age spots are clearly visible, and with a throaty voice and a broad New York accent, she tells the story of robbers who draw swastikas but who do not rob, of the real estate agents and the politicians who hire them, and she lists events and names names. As she talks, the mayor and council members avoid her eyes and the audience continues chattering, but Mona manages to go on, and she is smiling when she is through because the shadowy man turned his back on her while she was speaking, and now he is gone.

Others rise to voice support for J.C. and to castigate the mayor, and it is as though Mona never spoke, until ten past eleven when Ervina Boudreau, the librarian, comes to the podium. Everyone knows and respects Ervina, of course, and so she commands undivided attention when she says quite simply, "We must not act out of fear. Before reaching any decision, we must consider everyone's ideas." She turns to smile at Mona, then urges the council to appoint an independent commission to investigate the robberies, and especially Mona's allegations.

"Well, well. Isn't the world full of surprises," Dorothy says, poking Mona's arm with her elbow.

"I was afraid no one was listening," Mona whispers.

"I don't think they were listening, but they heard," Sam says.

"Girl, didn't you see J.C.?" Dorothy asks. "When you implicated him he jumped up like someone had stuck him in the behind. Oh, he sat down again without speaking. I think he had the good sense to realize that speaking out would only draw attention to your accusations."

Mona nods. "Did you see Shoemaker?"

"He's gone for good, dissolved." Sam is grinning. "He knows J.C.'s got to change his tactics. You have to remember, though, J.C.'s not going away."

"I know. He's been around for too long."

"Although now he's got someone to contend with," Sam adds.

"Right. And you'd better cover Ervina with glue and hug her tight to your bosom, honey."

"To remind J.C. that you're not alone anymore."

"And now maybe Adina will feel less threatened," Mona says. "I mean, seeing I'm not alone. Maybe she'll want me back."

A man sitting in the row behind them leans forward, singles out Dorothy, and tells her angrily, "Be quiet, lady."

At the same time murmurs of surprise erupt all around because the council has suddenly voted to hold another emergency meeting on Monday evening to consider Ervina's proposal.

41

FOG DRIFTS OUT from behind the walls, silver and blue, floating across the room and up to a gilded ceiling. A diamond-studded Christmas tree stands near the entrance, while Christmas music and slot machines tinkle in the background.

Dorothy is upstairs fine tuning the last chapter of her mystery novel before changing into her lucky blue dress, but Mona, still high from her success at the council meeting, has never been to Reno before and must see everything immediately: the mahogany game tables, the bald-headed croupiers, the dealers wearing green and red vests, and the people—so many people. In high heels, now wearing the gold lamé pantsuit, she hurries across the thick carpet.

She buys two rolls of quarters from the cashier who sits soberly behind golden bars. She makes her way to the heart of the slot-machine alcove where she watches others play for a while before deciding to try her luck at a poker machine. She used to play poker with Izzy and his friends and remembers the hands. The first roll of coins disappears quickly. She opens the second, plays more cautiously now, spits on each quarter before dropping it into the slot, listens intently as each one passes quietly into the great beyond.

Quite suddenly two quarters clink out into the chrome basin, two for one, she tells herself, her luck has turned. She whispers the Shema Yisrael—and says abra cadabra too—and almost immediately she is surrounded by an electronic symphony and exploding lights and an ever-growing mound of silver.

"Wait till Dorothy sees this. I think I broke the bank," Mona says aloud, although the other players do not seem to notice. She shovels the coins into her purse, then rushes across the room towards the hotel lobby. She is attracted to the Keno lounge, all decorated with fake tiger fur, and she sits down and begins filling out cards, just for herself, to see how well she would do if she were playing for money. Mostly though she stares into the liquid crystal numbers glowing softly on a huge board at the back wall, and at the colored fog forming itself into filmy animals. Bumblebees, porpoises, and raccoons float before her eyes, and now comes a long thin silver cloud. "Is that you here to scare me, John Shoemaker?" she murmurs, brushing the cloud away.

She dozes. She dreams she is at Sam's. There is the olive tree in place underneath the mirror tiles. Sad music fills the room—Uncle Gabe is playing his violin, hidden from view behind the branches. There is Lil climbing the tree. She is at the point where crown meets crown, passing from the tree of knowledge to the tree of life. Down below, dancing in circles, is John the Shoemaker, a skinny gnome. Adina and Gideon, with Ian and Andrew, emerge from an owl's hole deep inside the trunk. They say they will play musical chairs. Mona joins the game. When the music stops, she finds an empty chair. Gideon tries to butt her off. Lil and Uncle Gabe watch intently from the treetop, Dorothy and Sam from the kitchen transom. Gideon rolls up his sleeves, pushes with all his strength. Mona grabs hold of the rungs and refuses to let go. "You can't kick me out of my own cottage!" she shouts, and now she is awake, for a moment not knowing where she is, or why the man sitting next to her is staring.

She grabs up her purse and hugs it tightly to her chest as she hurries off towards the corridor leading to the hotel lobby, wondering how she ever considered moving out of her own home—what hope could there possibly be for Adina if she saw her own mother acting so timidly?

From on high, from behind the angels' singing, comes Lil's scratchy voice singing the song she sang for Mona so long ago: "Duma is at my right. Mefathiel is at my left. Aniel is at my feet. Lilith is at my head."

Mona looks up, half expecting to see a winged Lil flying down from the ceiling. "I'm Salome the Wandering Jew, Lil," Mona murmurs. "This is what I've learned. I'm the Queen of Sheba. I'm the Spanish dancer too, the black-haired dancer who came to my parents' bakery. I'm the fallen Sephardi with painted eyes."

Still hugging her purse to her chest, Mona hurries along until she must slow down because a trainload of tourists has just arrived and the corridor is jammed. At the same time something seems to be wrong with the hotel's fog-making machine. The red cloud billowing out from the walls is so thick she has to shield her eyes with her arm as she pushes through.

Quite suddenly the fog is behind her and she is standing in the hotel courtyard, a huge patio filled with fresh air and dazzling sunshine.

ABOUT THE AUTHOR

Harriet Ziskin has worked as a freelance journalist and as an education and civil rights specialist for the federal government. She also co-founded and directed Gateway Arts, a multi-cultural literary organization, and has been active in community groups. The character of Mona Pinsky was inspired by many of the people she met in her grassroots work.

Photo by Christine Delsol

Her short stories have been published in small press magazines, and her book, *The Blind Eagle*, a journalistic account of the criminal courts, has been widely used in college courses. She lives and writes in San Francisco.

Selected Titles from Award-Winning CALYX Books

NONFICTION

Natalie on the Street by Ann Nietzke. A day-by-day account of the author's relationship with an elderly homeless woman who lived on the streets of Nietzke's central Los Angeles neighborhood. *PEN West Finalist!*
ISBN 0-934971-41-2, $14.95, paper; ISBN 0-934971-42-0, $24.95, cloth.

The Violet Shyness of Their Eyes: Notes from Nepal by Barbara J. Scot. A moving account of a western woman's transformative sojourn in Nepal as she reaches mid-life. PNBA Book Award.
ISBN 0-934971-35-8, $14.95, paper; ISBN 0-934971-36-6, $24.95, cloth.

In China with Harpo and Karl by Sibyl James. Essays revealing a feminist poet's experiences while teaching in Shanghai, China.
ISBN 0-934971-15-3, $9.95, paper; ISBN 0-934971-16-1, $17.95, cloth.

FICTION

Killing Color by Charlotte Watson Sherman. These compelling, mythical short stories by a gifted storyteller delicately explore the African-American experience. Washington State Governor's Award.
ISBN 0-934971-17-X, $9.95, paper; ISBN 0-934971-18-8, $19.95, cloth.

Mrs. Vargas and the Dead Naturalist by Kathleen Alcalá. Fourteen stories set in Mexico and the Southwestern U.S., written in the tradition of magical realism.
ISBN 0-934971-25-0, $9.95, paper; ISBN 0-934971-26-9, $19.95, cloth.

Ginseng and Other Tales from Manila by Marianne Villanueva. Poignant short stories set in the Philippines. Manila Critic's Circle National Literary Award Nominee.
ISBN 0-934971-19-6, $9.95, paper; ISBN 0-934971-20-X, $19.95, cloth.

POETRY

The Country of Women by Sandra Kohler. A collection of poetry that explores woman's experience as sexual being, as mother, as artist. Kohler finds art in the mundane, the sacred, and the profane.
ISBN 0-934971-45-5, $11.95, paper; ISBN 0-934971-46-3, $21.95, cloth.

Light in the Crevice Never Seen by Haunani-Kay Trask. The first book of poetry by an indigenous Hawaiian to be published in North America. It is a revelation about a Native woman's love for her land, and the inconsolable grief and rage that come from its destruction.
ISBN 0-934971-37-4, $11.95, paper; ISBN 0-934971-38-2, $21.95, cloth.

Open Heart by Judith Mickel Sornberger. An elegant collection of poetry rooted in a woman's relationships with family, ancestors, and the world.
ISBN 0-934971-31-5, $9.95, paper; ISBN 0-934971-32-3, $19.95, cloth.

Raising the Tents by Frances Payne Adler. A personal and political volume of poetry, documenting a woman's discovery of her voice. Finalist, WESTAF Book Awards.
ISBN 0-934971-33-1, $9.95, paper; ISBN 0-934971-34-x, $19.95, cloth.

Black Candle: Poems about Women from India, Pakistan, and Bangladesh by Chitra Divakaruni. Lyrical and honest poems that chronicle significant moments in the lives of South Asian women. Gerbode Award.
ISBN 0-934971-23-4, $9.95, paper; ISBN 0-934971-24-2, $19.95 cloth.

Indian Singing in 20th Century America by Gail Tremblay. A brilliant work of hope by a Native American poet.
ISBN 0-934971-13-7, $9.95, paper; ISBN 0-934971-14-5, $19.95, cloth.

Idleness Is the Root of All Love by Christa Reinig, translated by Ilze Mueller. These poems by the prize-winning German poet accompany two older lesbians through a year together in love and struggle.
ISBN 0-934971-21-8, $10, paper; ISBN 0-934971-22-6, $18.95, cloth.

ANTHOLOGIES

The Forbidden Stitch: An Asian American Women's Anthology edited by Shirley Geok-lin Lim, et al. The first Asian American women's anthology. American Book Award.
ISBN 0-934971-04-8, $16.95, paper; ISBN 0-934971-10-2, $32, cloth.

Women and Aging, An Anthology by Women edited by Jo Alexander, et al. The only anthology that addresses ageism from a feminist perspective. A rich collection of older women's voices.
ISBN 0-934971-00-5, $15.95, paper; ISBN 0-934971-07-2, $28.95, cloth.

ORDER INFORMATION

CALYX Books are available to the trade from Consortium and other major distributors and jobbers.

Individuals may order direct from CALYX Books, P.O. Box B, Corvallis, OR 97339. Send check or money order in U.S. currency; add $2.00 postage for first book, $.75 each additional book.

CALYX, A Journal of Art and Literature by Women

CALYX, A Journal of Art and Literature by Women, has showcased the work of over two thousand women artists and writers since 1976. Committed to providing a forum for *all* women's voices, CALYX presents diverse styles, images, issues, and themes that women writers and artists are exploring.

"The work you do brings dignity, intelligence, and a sense of wholeness to the world. I am only one of many who bows respectfully—to all of you and to your work."
—Barry Lopez

"It is heartening to find a women's publication such as CALYX which is devoted to the very best art and literature of the contemporary woman. The editors have chosen works which create images of forces that control women; others extol the essence of every woman's existence."
—Vicki Behem, *Literary Magazine Review*

"Thank you for all your good and beautiful work."
—Gloria Steinem

Published in June and November; three issues per volume.

Single copy rate: $8.00.
Subscription rate for individuals: $18/1 volume.

CALYX Journal is available to the trade from Ingram Periodicals and other major distributors.

CALYX is committed to producing books of literary, social, and feminist integrity.

CALYX Journal is available at your local bookstore or direct from:

CALYX, Inc., PO Box B, Corvallis, OR 97339

CALYX, Inc., is a nonprofit organization with a 501(C)(3) status. All donations are tax deductible.